WARHORSES OF LETTERS

WARHORSES OF LETTERS

ROBERT HUDSON AND MARIE PHILLIPS

unbound

Warhorses of Letters
This edition first published in 2012
by Unbound
21 Peters Lane, Clerkenwell, London EC1M 6DS
www.unbound.co.uk

Text design and typesetting by Palindrome
Cover design and illustration by Tom Sears

A CIP record for this book
is available from the British Library

ISBN 978-1-908717-15-3

Printed in England by Clays Ltd, Bungay, Suffolk

CONTENTS

PREFACE

Dear Marengo,

We have been asked to write a preface to the first volume of our letters. I am really excited. Re-reading them massively takes me back to when I was less famous than you and all nervous!

I think the editors have done a really super job. I learnt loads of new things from the hoofnotes, although I still wish I knew what a Mameluke is. I suppose all humans just know that.

The only thing I worry about is that it might be weird that we are writing this in the present. Will it be weird, do you think?

KKH,

Copenhagen

~

Dear Copenhagen,

I, too, felt the hoof of history on my withers when I read back over our correspondence. Who could have thought that we, two of the most significant horses of the Napoleonic era, would go on to be two of the most significant horses of the twenty-first century as well? It is nice that you are finally as famous as me, although only one of us has our skeleton on display in Britain's National Army Museum. I hear that they did put a small lock of your hair in a temporary exhibition once.

Anyhow, given that we are horses writing letters, I doubt very much that writing in the present tense will be the thing that has people spitting out their tea.

To the readers of these humble words, I say: open your minds, open your hearts, you have nothing to lose but your reins.

Marengo
~

I agree.

Copenhagen
~

EXPLANATORY NOTE

This correspondence was first made public in the BBC Radio 4 series *Warhorses of Letters*. Space now allows us to present more complete versions of these exchanges, which we have supplemented with millions of learned hoofnotes. We have chosen to include the introductions from the radio series for no other reason than that we like them.

Expert readers will be surprised at the large number of factual facts they find within these letters. They will be surprised that the horses had such a clear view of their circumstances. They may think they notice lots of facts which are less factual, often much less factual. They may worry where the dividing line is. Our advice is, 'Don't worry, be happy.'

INTRODUCTION

Book, reader. Reader, book.

FOREWORD

is forearmed.

PROLOGUE

It was a sparkling January morning, frost heavy on the shelves of the String Theory Reading Room of the British Library. A yellowing leaf of aged paper corkscrewed through a shaft of dust-bemoted light. Marie Phillips, the tall, willowy, leonine, semi-eligible horsethropologist, gasped. With a scarlet talon she plucked it from the air moments before it shattered on the ground, and scanned the contents with eyes made for love, and also reading. Despite her signature Louboutins, impractical for library use perhaps, but indispensible weapons in the eternal struggle to be taken seriously as an academic, she stalked like a leopard through the reading room, scattering tattooed students and doddering professors with every step, taking care to shove the delicate scrap down her cleavage, partly to keep it safe, partly because this is the best way to steal things from the British Library.

After a short bus ride and longer tube journey, slightly delayed due to signal failure at Queen's Park, she ran, gasping, into the leather-book-lined study of her closest yet strictly platonic friend, the truculent, dwarfish, part-time cryptologist, part-time hockey commentator Dr Robert Hudson PhD.

'I've got it, I've got it!' she gasped.

'See a doctor,' he replied.

'Not that, you bumble-headed pygmy,' she gasped. 'The letters! The Copenhagen–Marengo letters! I know where they are!' she gasped.

'Please stop gasping,' he said.

'Then open a window,' she expostulated.

'And don't expostulate either. The cleaner's not coming until next week.'

He gazed into the crackling fire and ruminated awhiles. Suddenly, his one good eye lit up.

'What did you say?' he gasped. 'The Copenhagen and Marengo letters?'

'This yellowing leaf of aged paper tells us where to find them,' she said, yanking the note from her bosom and scoring a faint line of half-Irish, half-Hungarian blood across one alabaster hemisphere.

Dr Robert Hudson PhD rolled his one evil eye.

'How do you know what it says? It's in code.'

'You with your manly science. Sometimes there's a place for intuition.' She winked one of her two smoky eyes. 'Read the code. Tell me I'm wrong. And open a damn window, my eyes are really smoky.'

Dr Robert Hudson PhD read the code.

PROLOGUE

'You're wrong,' he said. 'It is just, as it appears to be, some string theory.'

A week later, quite by chance, they found the letters tucked behind the Ark of the Covenant at the British Museum's Fort William warehouse complex.

ABOUT THE EDITORS

Marie Phillips

A Galway beauty with a frosty heart, Marie never had any patience for the so-called ivory towers of academe. She has taught herself everything she needs to know and she did it the hard way. In 2004 she was the first westerner to goose the Dalai Llama and the year after that she ran a marathon even though it was raining. The only reason she isn't competing in the archery at the London Olympics is that it is taking place at Lord's and she refuses to play sport at a bastion of male-only privilege. You can tell her that women can be members there till you're blue in the face – she won't listen. She has a black belt. It is shiny.

She has made herself fluent enough in seven languages to pass as a native of Galway who speaks those languages, and she can read fourteen more. For fun, she once pretended to have met an unknown tribe in the forests of Belize who spoke the perfect language and to make the joke work properly she invented the perfect language, but it hasn't caught on. She can strip the engine of a vintage Benz in six minutes and her 1952 Vincent Black Lightning, *un petit cadeau* from legendary folk singer Richard Thompson, runs better than it did the day it was built. She wrote all the good episodes of Doctor Who.

Her academic field is microbiology. She is Head of Microbiology at the Open University, but she is a natural so it doesn't take up that much of her time.

She has been enveloped in the heady fug of horse-ography ever since the day after her disastrous first wedding to maverick astrologer Lord Rackamann of Rum. In an effort to stop her leaving him after learning, well, you know, he showed her the heart-rending private diary of Shergar (self-subtitled 'The Horse Who Hated Racing'). It bought Rackamann a week of her time and many men would die happily for less.

Her second husband, the still-dashing polo star Dino Ferranti (the unacknowledged inspiration for the character 'Dino Ferranti' in Jilly Cooper's *Polo*), finally taught her to accessorise and cook; her third was a lost cause and she doesn't speak about him.

In John Smith she found her fourth husband and, coincidentally, the love of her life. He it was who told her about the Copenhagen–Marengo letters. They were his life's quest, as they were Dr Robert Hudson PhD's. As you would imagine, John Smith and Dr Robert Hudson PhD, former best friends turned bitter rivals, became grudgingly respectful acquaintances again.

Marie is still married to Smith, in a kind of a way. On an ill-fated expedition to the Seriously Cold Weather Archive in northern Greenland, he was unfortunately entombed in a block of ice. It is possible that science might be able to revive him one day. Marie hopes this is the case but in the meantime the situation is very unsatisfactory.

Robert Hudson

Dr Robert 'Robbie' Hudson PhD (Cantab, revoked) was born plain old Robert Cornelius Wolf Hudson in Exeter, England, in whatever year it would take to make him thirty-eight years old when you are reading this. Exeter is the county city of the ceremonial county of Devon, with an estimated population of 119,600 and a lovely twelfth-century cathedral which may or may not hold the key to the final resting place of the last remaining piece of the True Cross.

Hudson's early childhood proved unremarkable, aside from a certain incident at the age of six, when his maternal uncle Rupert took him hiking in the Peruvian Andes and accidentally left him overnight on a freezing ridge. While not naturally careless, Rupert had been left with severe frostbite and memory loss after an encounter with a Saint Bernard (an actual saint, mystically preserved, not the breed of dog) and a bottle of blueberry schnapps. Although rescued by passing ornithologists, Hudson was bequeathed a lifelong terror of ice. Well the drinkers of Naples know the sight of his squat figure hurtling shrieking from bars where callow mixologists have not followed his exact specifications for a gin and tonic. This fear of ice rules him out as a possible suspect in the John Smith entombing, otherwise it would be pretty damn obvious who did it.

A child prodigy in a number of fields, Hudson was admitted to Apocryphal College, Cambridge University (an elite British academic institution founded in 1209), at the age of eight years old, to study Mathematics, More Mathematics, Philosophy, Cryptography, Zoology, Cryptozoology, Sports Sciences and Piano (and, as his musical career progressed, related melodic percussive instruments (glockenspiel, melodica and chromatic button accordion) though the organ, alas, always eluded him, due to his freakishly short legs.) Hudson excelled in every subject, and won blues in fifteen sports including Association Football, Rounders and Cage Fighting. Hudson became the youngest scholar ever to receive a PhD (at the age of twelve, thesis title: 'Black and White and Red All Over: Communist Zebra and the Kenyan Free Press') and went on to become an unpopular teacher.

He was expelled from Cambridge in disgrace at the age of seventeen after being recruited onto an undercover team of religious paranoiacs who believed that the wimple of the Virgin Mary was buried in the foundations of the ADC Theatre (founded 1855 by amateur dramaticians and supportive dentists). Falsely accused of terrorism after trying to blow up the theatre, Hudson spent several years in jail before spectacularly clearing his name when the wimple in question was found after the ADC was treated for dry rot and subsidence in whatever year would make sense here. Cambridge University, however, refused to reinstate him, and Hudson retreated into a life of bitterness, alcoholism and ranting calls to radio phone-in shows. It was following just such a late night call to talkSPORT (one of the United Kingdom's three analogue Independent National Radio broadcasters) that Hudson was offered the coveted position of Chief Hockey Correspondent, a role he still holds today. This finally gave him the financial freedom to pursue his lifelong obsession with the mythical, lost Copenhagen–Marengo letters, and he began to devote himself to their recovery.

Hudson's cryptographical expertise is much in demand, and he is often called away from his gay horse research to break codes and interpret symbols and stuff. Although ugly and bad-tempered, Hudson exudes an animal sex appeal. In spite of this, he manages to attract the lust and admiration of some young research assistant or other on every mission, although the relationships always come to an unspecified end in between assignments. He has never married. This is fine in men.

How do we know that animals have not a language of their own? My opinion is that it is a presumption in us to say no, because we do not understand them. A horse has memory, knowledge and love.

NAPOLEON

Being born in a stable does not make one a horse.

WELLINGTON

PACKET 1

THE FORT WILLIAM LETTERS

A few months ago, two maverick academics cataloguing an extraordinary collection of ephemera discovered in the British Museum's Fort William warehouse complex, in a neglected room with the yellowing label, 'Tat We Shouldn't Have Bought and Are Now Legally Unable to Get Rid Of', made an extraordinary find – a packet of letters which casts an extraordinary new light on one of the most extraordinary chapters in our island race's extraordinary story. We will let these extraordinary epistles speak for themselves. The year is February 1810.

1

Dear Marengo brackets Napoleon's horse close brackets,

I've never written a letter like this before.* You probably

---

* Shortly after the broadcast of the Copenhagen–Marengo correspondence, J. Danforth Quayle, former vice-president of the United States (1989–93) and a keen amateur horsologist, wrote excitedly to tell us that the Marengo letter was, and we quote, 'my White Grail, my Holy Whale, whatever you want to call it.' Apparently, Mr Quayle has a collection of letters from Copenhagen, all written in early 1810, all beginning 'I've never written a letter like this before.' For instance, 'Dear Pope (winner of the Epsom Derby), I've never written a letter like this before. You probably get hundreds of them and I imagine a horse version of your secretary or agent will never let you see this anyway, but I would never forgive myself if I didn't send it. I have seen pictures of you. You are literally an oil painting. I don't know how you could look so amazing with that titchy little Robert Robson on your back.' Or, rather more elegiacally, 'Dear Sir Peter Teazle, I've never written a letter like this before. You probably get hundreds of them, mostly from your many, many successful offspring, but I would never forgive myself if I didn't send it. I have heard that you never smile when you are getting mares with foals and I wondered if, after such a successful career at stud, you might think that a change is as good as a rest. I am not offering a rest, but I am offering a change, wink.' Copenhagen also wrote to the warhorses of Blücher and Marshall Ney. Perhaps the most amusing piece in Mr Quayle's collection, and the letter which first piqued his interest, is a framed note he stole from one of the lavatories in the White House. It is written by Copenhagen to 'America', which he wrongly believed to be the name of King George III's horse. Actually, Copenhagen was labouring

3

get hundreds of them and this one might never arrive anyway, because of the war smiley face,[*] but I would never forgive myself if I didn't send it and so here it is. I have seen pictures of you. You are literally an oil painting. I don't know how you could look so amazing with that dumpy Napoleon on your back.

My name is Copenhagen because I am out of Lady Catherine who was in foal with me at the Battle of Copenhagen, which is ironic because I am not a warhorse but you are. I am dark brown and I am by John Bull, out of a mare by the Rutland Arabian, and also by Meteor, who was the son of the mighty Eclipse. You are an Arabian too, aren't you? Maybe we are distant cousins even! That doesn't matter for horses of course. I am only two and you are at least twelve, but that also doesn't matter for horses, as you know. Anyway, people tell me I look older than two.[†]

I am a racehorse. It is so lucky that I didn't become a warhorse, or we'd have been mortal enemies, and that would be a nightmare. The word nightmare always makes me think of lady horses that want to seduce me. Lady horses, or mares, are always trying to seduce me.

---

under a misapprehension created by a famous cartoon, drawn at the time of the American Revolution, in which George is bucked from a horse, labelled 'America'. In this cartoon, the horse 'America' represents America and not a horse.

[*] Horse smiley faces are not drawn the same as human smiley faces. They are elongated and have ears. Also, horses cannot smile.

[†] Even for horses, two is a bit young.

They don't get very far.

Maybe you are only interested in lady horses brackets mares close brackets, but when I saw the pictures, my equine gaydar pointed due south wink.*

I hope you reply. Love,

Copenhagen, kiss kiss hoofprint

∽

Dear Copenhagen,

What a rare pleasure to receive a letter from a frisky young thing such as yourself. You are quite mistaken to believe that I am the recipient of many such overtures. The pasture of fame is a lonely one,† as very few have the courage to approach an animal of my standing.‡ It

---

* The equine gaydar is a myth but nobody knows what it is a myth of. For horses, a myth is as good as a mile.

† Marengo is quoting the character of Old Agamemnon, the donkey who becomes mayor of Horsetown in the great satire Animal Village by the eighteenth-century Scottish author, Horsey McGorsey (out of Spatchcock by Tantara). It seems likely that Marengo does not realise that Old Agamemnon is the most likely model for the English saying, 'a pompous ass'.

‡ Tech-savvy sleuth Lynette Sherburne notes that while Marengo has a full Wikipedia entry with picture, Copenhagen has nothing. (The horse, that is. Copenhagen the city has an absurdly long entry. It is only the capital of Denmark.) We do not know the reason, but we can speculate. Copenhagen is exactly the kind of horse who would write a Wikipedia entry for his lover but would not write one for himself. Marengo is the type of horse who would write

is one of the great sadnesses of my position, and I am moved that you have written to break my isolation, and with such rare enthusiasm.

I must, however, correct you on a few misapprehensions.

You speak with generosity of my appearance, but the pictures do flatter. Most importantly, I am not, in fact, a horse. At 14 hands 1 inch only, I am technically a pony,* though I am taller with my mane fluffed up. This has put off suitors in the past and I will understand if you are amongst them.

Equally, it is with some pain that I note your reference to my dear Napoleon as 'dumpy'. He and I are perfectly to scale. Napoleon, I am sure, does not have a fair reputation on the racecourses of Britain, but my affection for him could not be greater, indeed I am proudly branded with his initial, and a crown, just above my gaskin. Know that if we are to pursue this correspondence I will never renounce Mr Napoleon. He has too much need of me. I must admit I am concerned about my master. He should be brimming with happiness and pride. He is the greatest military leader the world has ever seen! But ever since he was excommunicated, he has been moping. He and the Pope were involved in a dispute over who owns Rome. Napoleon told the Pope to go to Paris and the Pope told

---

about himself on Wikipedia.

* By convention, Arab horses are never classified as ponies, no matter how short they are. It is one of the reasons the rest of the horse world finds them so unbearably pretentious.

Napoleon to go to Hell. I do not think that Napoleon would mind Hell so very much, he is the bravest of men, but he needed the Pope to divorce him from that buck-toothed *putain* Josephine. So he kidnapped the Pope, and the church had a mysterious change of heart and granted the divorce, but now Mr Napoleon does not know what to do with him. It is all a little embarrassing.

Now now, this is all terribly serious, and you a mere lad of two. I do apologise. My dear Copenhagen, I very much hope that none of this causes you to reconsider your regard. I confess I was quite delighted with your letter, and the sentiments within. Your lively manner appeals to me greatly, I cannot say how greatly. And it is with some relief that I note you are a racehorse, as it would be much to my distress were we to meet on opposing sides on the battlefields of Europe.

With warmth and hope,

Marengo

∾

Dear Marengo,

When I got your letter I was like, oh my horsey god.[*]

---

[*] The horsey god is, in many ways, similar to the human Judeo-Christian godhead: omniscient, omnipotent, benevolent, male, white,[**] etc., as well as equally baffling in terms of divine intervention (or not), and allowing the existence of evil (colic, French butchers). Horsey heaven is notably different from human heaven, however. It has fewer harps

[**] Technically grey.

You are amazing with words, I had to use a dictionary for 'excommunicated'. Don't worry I am not stupid, it's just I have always had to put book learning second place to my athletic career. Racing is bloody amazing, and it's all I've ever wanted to do, but is a difficult environment to be a gay horse in it is testosterone everywhere you look. Presumably it's even worse for warhorses. Thank the horsey god, again, that I am not one.

Also, don't worry, I am not a size queen, smiley face. In fact my first was a pony, he was called Twinkle. He told me that I have a very strong tail which is something gay horses use to do something it would be impossible to describe how nice it is to humans.* Horse heaven only knows what tricks you have learnt in all your years of experience, it makes me excited just to think about it.

Anyway, you were so honest about your size so I must be totally honest too. However hard I train, which is bloody hard quite frankly, I do not have a great turn of speed. Yesterday, I ran the quarter-mile in 30 seconds, like some kind of donkey.† All the other

---

and a lot more grass. The horsey Messiah is yet to come, although horsey Messianic sects are common. It is believed that Marengo was briefly a member of such a sect during his early adolescence, before becoming disenchanted after the world failed to end on New Year's Eve 1799/80, and moving into horsey atheism.

* We have not figured out what this is. Believe us, we have tried.

† To contextualise, the great Secretariat, in his Triple Crown year of 1973, won the Kentucky Derby in a time

horses laughed at me. I'm really stressed about it.

I am a stayer though brackets not just in races wink close brackets and I hope that I will break into longer races after this year when I am officially three, even though I am a young three, because you have to remember that all horses get arbitrarily given the same birthday which is January the first. Oh, wait, you don't have to remember because you are also a horse.

I will not be horrible about Napoleon again. It is not being horrible to him to say that in the pictures of you, he is not the one that makes me have to lie down on cold wet grass or I would have an accident.

I hope he is feeling better but I worry that if he is you will have to go to war in the peninsula. Our top guy there is called Viscount Wellington. My stablemate Thunderclap out of Stormfront by Death to the French – I'm sorry but that's his name – is obsessed with wars. He's totally jealous I am called after a battle, actually. He says it is an insult to the memory of the fallen that I am not more patriotic.

Anyway, I used to think Thunderclap was cool

---

of under two minutes. His first quarter-mile took 25½ seconds, his last quarter-mile took 23 seconds. Secretariat was unusually fast, but 30 seconds is rubbish, whoever you are. Incidentally, racehorses aren't as fast as the American Quarter Horse which is bred to sprint, and which has reached speeds of 55 mph. The Internet says that; we haven't measured it ourselves.

There is a song called 'The Fastest Horse in a One Horse Town', by Billy Ray Cyrus, but it isn't about horses. It's about motor racing.

because he's by far the beta horse in our stable, and, as you know, the horse alphabet starts with beta.* Thunderclap came second in the 1,000 Guineas last year. He finished moments after his half-brother Lightning out of Storm Front by You Canna Change The Laws of Physics, but all he ever does is tease me for being slow. He's not cool, he's a bully.

The thing is, it is hard to ignore him because he is so bloody beta all the time. He says Wellington is amazing and all the French will be inevitably crushed. I'm scared that you will be hurt. That makes me sound silly, doesn't it?

I bet it does. I'm sorry. Anyway, it was amazing to hear from you, and I am literally pawing the ground with impatience dreaming of your reply.

Love,

Copenhagen kiss hoofprint kiss kiss

〜

Dear Copenhagen,

My heart leapt like a foal in springtime when I received your latest. I confess I was filled with apprehension lest news of my, shall we say, vertical limitations, were to prove insurmountable to you, but it would seem you find them quite mountable indeed, so to speak. I blush to write such a thing. It is not my custom to be so

---

* Equine graphologists have so far confirmed the existence of 427 letters in the horse alphabet, but more are coming to light every day.

THE FORT WILLIAM LETTERS

forward, but dare I say that you inspire me?

Thank you for your kind concern regarding Mr Napoleon. I am glad to say that he is in much higher spirits. I am certain that it is because he is spending more time in the saddle. I am working hard to improve Napoleon's riding. He has an almost total lack of – we call it – '*elegance*'. I think it is because his centre of gravity is unusually low. But I would rather be poorly ridden and well understood. Of course best of all is to be well-understood and well-ridden, and thus my thoughts turn to your youthful vigour, dear Copenhagen.

I expect us to join the peninsular war at any moment. I am taking Spanish lessons in anticipation.* Do not worry that I will get hurt; it is the risk, and the glory, of combat. Also I have heard of some excellent bio-oils for reducing the appearance of scar tissue. I would not usually believe in such remedies, but these oils are extracted from snakes.†

---

* Spanish is one of the hardest languages for a horse to speak, because of the bilabial fricatives.

† The snake oil was to prove a disappointment to Marengo, as this letter, discovered folded into a tiny square to prop up a wobbly table leg at London's legendary Bob Bob Ricard restaurant, demonstrates:

Dear Dr Miracle,
I am writing to complain about your snake oil. It contains the wrong kind of snakes.
   *Proper Chinese snake oil should be extracted from the Chinese water snake (*Enhydris Chinensis*), a creature rich in essential fatty acids including eicosapentaenoic acid*

The Emperor is filled with energy, his compact little body leaping about all over the place. Also, he is more constipated than usual, a sure sign that we will soon be going into battle.

Thunderclap out of Stormfront by Death to the French sounds as stupid as his name. In war, there is no prize for coming second. And he is extraordinarily poorly informed. Your British army holds no fears for my Napoleon, who refers to Wellington as 'that terrified leopard'. We will push the leopard out from the cat flap of Spain!*

(EPA), an omega 3 acid found in higher concentrations in said snake than in its more popular source the salmon, and renowned for its healing properties.

Your snake oil appears to be extracted from the inferior EPA-poor red or black rattlesnake.

Thus, although your oil has provided some small topical relief for my rheumatism, neuralgia, sciatica, lame back, lumbago, contracted cords, toothache, sprains, swellings, frostbite, chilblains, sore throat and insect bites, I found it completely ineffective for the purpose for which I made the purchase, viz, unsightly scars.

Please send a refund by return of post.

Yours sincerely,

Marengo
(Warhorse to the Emperor Napoleon Bonaparte)
PS Has your supply of Bach's Rescue Remedy been restocked yet?

* In 1953 Mexican–American telecoms engineer Alfonso Cuarez patented the horseflap for householders who wished to share their homes with their beloved equines, without the

But enough war talk. Do not be concerned about your lack of velocity. Such things mean nothing to me. You describe yourself as a 'stayer' – clearly you are a horse of valour – on the battlefield this would make you a prize indeed. But you are not a warhorse and I can barely imagine the life that you lead, one of sport and play and healthy competition. Pray tell me more of the racecourses of England. To picture your lithe young fetlocks pounding the turf causes me quite the distraction.

Yours, very distracted indeed,

Marengo

Dear M,

The racecourses of England are muddy and wet, and the racehorses of England are shits. I returned to my stable yesterday to find that Thunderclap out of Stormfront by Death to the French had pinned a picture of you covering (the horse word for having sex with) Napoleon and him smiling. I would have been smiling if it was me but I know that's different.

Thunderclap out of Stormfront by Death to the French says that Napoleon is not fighting in the Peninsular War because he is scared. He says that Napoleon is a show pony, and does not have any bottom, the contemporary word for courage and durability.

---

hassle of having to keep getting up to let them in and out of the garden. It has yet to catch on.

13

My trainer is still disappointed with me, but I am determined that this will change. The other horses like Thunderclap out of etc. think the kind of horse we are – i.e. gay – is all flash and no bottom, but I am a stayer not a sprinter. I will show them all my bottom in the end, ha ha.*

---

* Radio 4 listener Rachel Holdsworth asked if horses such as Copenhagen and Marengo (i.e. gay) faced problems with being outed in the media. It is about to become a slightly less little-known fact that *The Horse Times* and *Cheval* were both established in the early nineteenth century by gay horses. These papers of record didn't push a radical agenda, but they played an enormous part in maintaining a civilised discourse of equine sexuality, simply by presenting gay horses as normal, which they are. On the other hand, both papers were Jingoistic and bloody intrusive when it came to any hint of cross-channel fraternisation, and while Copenhagen and Marengo were never publicly outed, no one whose heart is not made of a massive icicle will ever forget the story of the French mare Heliotrope (Lieutenant Colonel Jean-Antony Fragonard) and the English stallion Buccaneer (Trooper the Honourable Ruddington Plover). Their relationship was made public early in The Hundred Days and after weeks of protestations that they would not let their personal feelings stand in the way of their duty, they decided that the pain of their comrades' distrust was more than they could bear and, as the opening salvos of Waterloo fired, they charged towards each other across an otherwise empty battlefield, ready to die in a mangled hail of bullets. Every horse present knew what was happening and felt guilty, and not a horse present was dry-eyed when, after their respective owners died in the mangled hail of bullets,

I wonder how we will ever meet since I am a race horse and you are a warhorse? Thank god I am not a warhorse though. I can't repeat that often enough.

Impatiently,

Copenhagen

～

Dear Copenhagen,

So it turns out that those Spanish lessons were a complete waste of time. We are not going to the peninsula. I have written to Castanet, Don Miguel Ricardo de Alvara y Esquivel's reserve saddle horse, cancelling the rest of our sessions. *Ay carumba!* Which is Spanish for *zut alors!* I doubt I will ever leave the Tuileries again. Napoleon has sent André Masséna to fight the war in Spain in his place. He said 'keep an eye on things for me' which annoyed Masséna greatly, because he only has one eye: Napoleon shot the other one out by mistake. As for Napoleon, on those rare occasions that he gets out of the bath, he comes to my stable and scratches me behind the ears, saying I am a good old boy. Old! I am not ready for dog meat yet. But I suppose you racehorses know all about premature decrepitude. Perhaps you even have certain secret techniques or remedies to extend your vitality. These would be of no relevance to me, of course, but the subject interests me. On an academic level.

Heliotrope and Buccaneer cantered together into a Belgian forest, never to be seen again.

You and your bottom should not give Thunderclap another thought. With his doctored pictures and his jibes he is certainly paying you plenty of attention. I believe that he is envious of our correspondence – a sentiment I abhor. What does he look like?

Vigorously,

Marengo

~

Dear M,

I thought that your letter was really open, and I was honoured you were able to confide your insecurities in me. I think it is an important moment in our relationship.

My insecurities are about racing. I ran yesterday, for the tenth time this year, and came third from last. If I keep this up, I'll be turned into glue. Thunderclap said it's as if my hooves are made of glue already. Sometimes I feel like he's right. Thunderclap told me I would stay young if I ate rotten turnips,* which are the most disgusting taste possible for horses, but it turned out he was joking.

Luckily, you are grey, so no one will ever notice that you are old.

Love,

C

---

* Things horses don't like the taste of, in reverse order: 5. Snails 4. Colonel Bogey 3. The air in a slaughterhouse on a late spring day 2. Success OR failure 1. Rotten turnips

PS Thunderclap is exactly my height, and he is mid-night black with a quiff in his mane which he doesn't have to do anything to to keep curly. It's wasted on him.

～

Esteemed Copenhagen,

I was a little confused by your letter as I don't have any insecurities. But I am glad that you feel you can share all of yours with me. Do not listen to Thunderclap. In fact I think it would be better if you never spoke to him again, or looked at him.

I dreamed of you last night. We were racing together – clearly in my dream I flattered myself with unrealistic fleetness of foot – and I knew we were on an English racecourse because of the rain and pervasive smell of haddock.* You were just ahead of me. There was, incidentally, no sign of Thunderclap. Your ripe muscles were pulling taut the skin of your hindquarters, your lush tail was swishing, and oh, the movement of your strong, provocative legs . . . But, at that moment, I awoke, and the sound of your hooves drumming the grass was just the distant drum of drumming. I have not had such a dream since I was a heady colt. It must be because I had rotten turnips just before going to sleep.

In any case it was a rude awakening, although not as rude as I would have liked. Copenhagen, I have the worst possible news. Napoleon has a new mare to

---

* Horses are unique in the animal kingdom in being able to identify all breeds of fish by their smell.

ride. I speak figuratively. Napoleon would never ride any horse other than me, aside from his other saddle horses, but I am his favourite.

What I mean is that Napoleon is married. We have not gone to war because he was too busy thinking about flower arrangements and colour schemes and party favours for the bridesmaids. His new wife is a Hapsburg, an eighteen-year-old filly called Marie Louise who can speak six languages but is too frightened to walk behind a horse in case it kicks. She tried to annex my affections with sugar lumps, but I am not so easily bought.

Be glad that you are a racehorse, you with your most excellent bottom. For as long as races are run, you will be gainfully employed. Do not fear the glue factory. Although we are in different countries and I have never met you and am not entirely clear where you live, I will protect you, I promise it.

For my part, I fear this marriage means that I will be retired to give pony rides to squealing brats on the shingles of Nice. Nice is not nice*. Actually it is quite nice but I thought that was funny. You will now be wondering why I did not do the joke 'Nice is nice'. I am wondering this myself.

Yearningly, yes, yearningly,

Marengo

---

* Horses are the only animals who like puns. Humans, for instance, think they are asinine.

18

THE FORT WILLIAM LETTERS

Dear Marengo,

The Viscount Wellington has bought me. I am to be a warhorse. I will never race again and I will have to go to war, and it's the Napoleonic Wars, basically, and our owners are, well, you know, and oh my horsey God, do we have to be arch-enemies now? Is this the end? I wish –

And there the letters abruptly end. We have heard, however, that there might be a further packet in the National Gallery miscatalogued as 'Virginia Woolf: Racist Political Cartoons and Other Juvenilia'. We can but hope.

PACKET 2

THE VIRGINIA WOOLF LETTERS

Hello again. We are following the extraordinary corres-pondence between the racehorse Copenhagen and the Emperor Napoleon's favourite saddlehorse, Marengo. In the first packet of these letters, we saw the tentative beginnings of an attachment. They concluded abruptly in 1810 with Copenhagen distraught to learn that he had been bought by Wellington, and was henceforth to become a warhorse. He assumed the Napoleon-loyal Marengo would now hate him. This second packet of letters, run to earth in the National Gallery in a folder miscatalogued as 'Virginia Woolf: Racist Political Cartoons and Other Juvenilia', takes up the story.

21

Dear Marengo,

Oh my horsey God! You are totally amazing for not minding that I have become a warhorse even though you have been fighting the English for years.* I don't

---

* Concerned horse-lover Luke O'Shea writes:

I have a dear, dear Arabian mare called Blackie, who sadly was shunned by her horsey community when she started courting her sabino friend Snowy. What practical advice would Copenhagen and Marengo offer from a nineteenth-century Anglo-French cultural perspective to my young lady horse in love, in dealing with horsey race prejudice in modern Britain. I am at a loss as to know how to console her.

Marengo replies:

Dear Luke,
After much discussion between us, Copenhagen and I have decided that it is I, Marengo, who am to answer your question. The reason for this is twofold. First of all, though he denies it, the only race that Copenhagen really knows about are his old racing days, and we have all heard enough about those. Second, Copenhagen does not like to see himself as an agony aunt. He thinks that aunts are old and fusty. Well! I am not so old or fusty myself! And also, horse biology being what it is, aunts can be quite young and cool, in fact most horses have many, many aunts, a large number of which may actually be younger than themselves, so it is not all repetitive stories about days of yore and complaining about modern music not really being music. Quite the contrary! Although I have no time for this R and B the twenty-first century seems so fond of. In my day, if you could sing, you could sing. There was none of this autotune

---

nonsense. *There was a charger in our regiment, by name of Milord, who had such a voice, it was like horsey angels (if such a thing were to exist, which they do not) were weeping down his throat! If only you could have heard him!* Hélas, *he was shot in the neck at Austerlitz and his voice was never quite the same afterwards. Also, he has been dead for two hundred years.*

To your problem. As a human (I assume that you are a human) you conflate the different categories of horse race, to whit: breed, nationality, and colour. From the unimaginative human naming, I assume that Blackie is 'black' (in fact probably a dark chestnut or bay, mistaken by a novice) and Snowy is white (presumably, from your letter, a sabino-white, not dominant-white, and well done to you for being able to tell the difference). This does not matter to horses, except palominos, who think they are superior and refuse to breed with anyone else, and so nobody else wants to bang them anyway.

Blackie being an Arab and Snowy a sabino may be more of an issue. You do not tell me what breed Snowy is, but as Arabs never carry the sabino gene, we can class him or her as non-Arab. As an Arab myself – although I have been called a Barb, I assure you I am not a Barb, this is English propaganda – I can tell you that by no means all Arabs are dating snobs, even though we are often tarred with that brush. How could we be, when we have been deliberately interbred with inferior breeds, in order to bestow on them our speed, endurance, strength and refinement? However, it may be that Blackie's circle is of a particularly stuck-up variety.

But I suspect that Blackie and Snowy's respective nationalities is where the true problem lies. Horses are not, on the whole, racist in terms of breed or colour, but they are the most terrible xenophobes. Ah, the difficulties Copenhagen

really care about Viscount Wellington or who wins the war. The whole you-win-we-lose thing seems really confrontational and hacho, which is the horse word for macho,* as you know. I don't mind that you care who wins, though. It's cute, like everything about you.

I can tell between the lines that you are stressed about Napoleon's wedding. Don't be stressed. There

---

and I went through with our love across the barricades! (Or behind the ridges, that being more Wellington's thing.) Many of our compatriots were quite unable to forgive what they saw as our betrayal of our countries, and I am ashamed to admit that I almost let Copenhagen slip through my horseshoes out of an unwillingness to accept his misguided loyalty to perfidious Albion. I now understand that this is merely a lovable quirk. As Blackie and Snowy are both Anglo-Saxon names, I can only assume that one out of the pair originates in the northern half of the American continent, or, worse, somewhere in the Antipodes, where horses scuffle around in the dust all day chasing rabbits and saying things like 'Mate'. It is of no matter. Love is blind, and also selectively deaf.

Your answer is simple. It is Blackie who must shun her so-called 'community' and make better friends, who are willing to accept her and Snowy for who they are and their love for the rare and beautiful thing that it is. As for how to console her, might I suggest some Polo mints.

Yours, encouragingly,
Marengo

---

* The song 'So Macho' by Sinitta (1986) is a straight copy of 'So Hacho' by Spearmint out of Maisie by Bartleby (1985). All horses think Sinitta is a bitch.

are loads of princesses who are all basically the same, but there is only one Marengo and there is only one Napoleon Bonaparte. You are made for each other, and one of you is also made for me.

Incidentally, the first thing I learnt when I got here was that Wellington has lost twelve horses in the first three years of the Peninsular War. This seemed really weird, and I asked the other horses where they thought the lost horses were? They looked at me funny and then I got it. So, I'm going to die soon.

Since my last letter, we have had a victory at a place called Bussaco in Portugal due to Wellington's usual ruse of hiding some men behind a ridge, and we've been riding around in the dust looking at forts he's building and I'll tell you what it all is: bo-ring.

I really miss being a racehorse. At the time I hated all the galloping and so on, but you forget how much you grow to depend on the release of endorphins.

Everyone says I have picked up being a warhorse really fast, though, like it's hard. All you have to do is not jump when a cannon goes off.* But that doesn't mean I

---

* Equine Militarologist Alistair Huston asks whether it was really so simple. Of course it wasn't, Copenhagen is being modest. As historians never cease to point out, the training received by British warhorses in the nineteenth century has formed the model for human military training ever since. Thus, on first arriving at the stable, a scruffy civilian horse would be met by the most useless, overweight, unmotivated old nag the cavalry was still keeping in oats. For the safety of others, this horse was kept as far away from the field of battle as possible, and hence had been seconded to the receiving centre.

This fat and self-important horse would carry out what it claimed were vital and difficult tests, failure to pass which would probably indicate that the new recruit was a hundred years old or only had three legs.

Humans take fourteen weeks to pass through the Common Military Syllabus, which is based on a course horses used to take in fourteen days, at the end of which they were fully de-civilianised. Liberal media elite horses who don't understand anything will say this is brutal and dehorseising but they are basing this on tens of thousands of isolated incidents. As Copenhagen later wrote in a lecture to young warhorses, 'It's not a holiday camp, but it's meant to make you, not break you.' It was a very boring lecture.

Many of the horses arrive young (one or two) and they have never cooked or ironed a shirt for themselves. They leave without having done those things too, but at least they have been trained to be warhorses – they have learned Skill at Arms, which is how to hold your back when your rider is trying to smash someone in the face with a sword, and Fieldcraft, which is how to camouflage yourself as a tree, which is bloody hard if you're a horse. They also learn such jargon as sitrep (situation report), locstat (location status) and Roger That (not what Copenhagen first thought it was). Basic training is physically very hard, with lots of being cold and miserable on Welsh mountains and being told it is nothing by a tireless horse three times your age who served in an Alpine winter. You learn to trust your fellows in a way you have never had to trust any other horse, and you know who are the very, very few 'jack bastards' in your intake, who you will hate for the rest of your life because they are moral cowards who only ever looked after themselves. The usual thing they do is steal your nut ration and pretend they didn't. When this happens you want to kick them in the

---

muzzle, you really bloody do.

After basic, you go to train for your specific role, be it being an intelligence horse and learning French and getting deliberately captured and pretending not to mind and then being given to a stupid French officer and sending back messages about troop movements or, as Copenhagen was, being sent to dressage school so he could walk in parades and not embarrass his boss.

Also, as a senior officer's horse, Copenhagen would have faced two weeks at Aintree, the equine equivalent of Sandhurst, whose assault course was later turned into a race-track. This was intended to make you feel like you were part of the decision-making process. (You are really not part of the decision-making process if you are a horse.) Warhorses have one of two recollections of 'The Factory' as they call Aintree. They loved or they hated it. There is no middle ground, unlike with Marmite which most people have finally agreed is something that almost everyone who ever expresses an opinion on the subject thinks they are unusual for being able to take or leave.

One of the most important lessons Aintree teaches, about war and life, is that no plan survives contact with the enemy. There is a notice board called the Dear John board, and every time a horse got a Dear John letter, they would pin it up for all to see. It sounds like it would be humiliating, but it wasn't. It would be wrong to call it a badge of pride, either, it was just a recognition that you were now a different horse.

The horse equivalents of colour sergeants are excellent and colourful, and mainly drum into their soft trainees that their job is to follow bloody orders. They tend to be big on malapropisms ('Conjugate on the other side of the wall', 'Excavate the stables', 'I am pacifically talking to you, my foal'). No one is sure whether they are doing it deliberately,

am not scared, and something about being nearly about to die all the time makes me frisky. Is this normal?

I am going to try something. OK. Right. I'm embarrassed because you are from France and experienced and I am just a big, handsome racehorse with amazing muscle definition and huge eyelashes, and now I am walking slowly towards you, whinnying gently to let you know I am aroused, and now I am approaching with my head low to signify submission, even though that's not my style, and now I am nibbling your ears and stroking your flank with my strong tail and, oh god, is this embarrassing and crap? I was trying something, but it's not a very English thing to try. If it interests you, and you reply, then maybe I could try better next time.

Kiss kiss hoofprint,

Your Copenhagen

~

Why Copenhagen,

Really you make me very, very cross. There is so much more to being a warhorse than not jumping when the cannons go off. I am approaching you with a crop and spurs – you are wearing leather blinkers but at the sound of me you start to quiver – the whip comes down on your saucy waggling rump – your neigh is a mixture of pain and exquisite pleasure – a ha ha! Do you see what you I am doing here? I am pretending to be cross

---

especially the last one, which can be taken both ways.

so that I can invent a sexy sado-masochistic scenario!
Do you like it? I liked yours very much. You say you are
not fast but you seem pretty fast to me! May I check,
fast is English slang for sexually willing, yes?[*]

Of course, there is no more to being a warhorse than
not jumping when the cannons go off.[†] And also not

---

[*] Yes.

[†] French horse training was much less enlightened, obviously. It was all run by people rather than horses. Marengo
would have been treated to a brutal toughening-up regime and
taught to survive on dry rations (it doesn't take any teaching –
you are just given dry rations and you survive on them).

One of the aims of this brutality was to make horses immune to the traumas of battle. Trainers played drums, un-
sheathed swords in the horses' faces, all that sort of thing.
Humans seemed not to realise that the trauma horses wanted
to be immune from was the blunt force trauma caused by
cannon balls, etc., and the training did nothing about that.

As for Marengo's special training: Napoleon's valet
Constant wrote, 'It was necessary that, in the midst of the
fastest gallop – Napoleon favoured only that kind of pace –
the horse was able to come to a dead stop.' This was because
Napoleon liked to stop suddenly during gallops so all his
Marshalls also had to stop. One of them would inevitably be
taken by surprise and fall off. Napoleon found this hilarious.
He never tired of it.

Napoleon also demanded that his horses could do the sort
of tricks horses could do in circuses. It was unnecessary, but
Napoleon loved circuses. If he had become a clown, they
say, the whole history of Europe would have been different.
They are right.

Sometimes, to habituate them to the surprises of battle,

minding when you step on dead people. They squelch beneath the hooves. *Hélas*, now I am no longer in the mood for horseplay.

You will not believe it but there IS another Napoleon Bonaparte! Napoleon's new filly has foaled already. The problem with Josephine was not her poor hygiene but her lack of issue. They have christened this child Napoleon, which is vainglorious, and also what I was hoping to call my firstborn foal, should I ever have one. Now I cannot without looking like a copy-horse. They have also given him the soubriquet the King of Rome, which is stupid. He has never even been to Rome. But Napoleon cannot resist winding up the Pope. I call him Nappy 2. You will think me fanciful, but the baby resembles that great British general the Duke of Marlborough, John Churchill. Except for without the big curly wig, if you can imagine such a thing as a tiny bald Churchill. But I think this is just coincidence. Napoleon would not allow himself to be cuckolded by a fat English general of a previous era.

Napoleon dotes on Nappy 2. I cannot see why. Human babies cannot walk for an entire year after they are born, they make terrible sounds constantly, and always, always have one liquid or another coming from the eyes or mouth or private parts, although for

---

trainers fired guns while horses were eating their oats. This was a stupid move. Horses do not eat oats in the middle of battles. It was totally pointless. Coincidentally or not, the French lost in the end.

a horse, of course, no parts are private.* Horses are evidently far superior, so why does Napoleon no longer linger in the stables the way he used to? I heard him call Nappy 2 *Mon Petit Pamplemousse*, which used to be his nickname for me.

Luckily, I have some good news. We are soon to begin marching on Russia, and will leave the squalling bundle far behind. I like the sound of Russia. It is a place of music and passion. We will kick their butts.

Dasvidania! That is Russian for goodbye.

Marengo

⌒

Dear Marengo,

The start of your letter was bloody wow! But also you talked about Napoleon's issue issue and now I am going to say something difficult but honesty is very important, isn't it? I am confused but I am sure it is nothing.

A lady warhorse called Eve's Apple out of Serpent by Normal is Best keeps wanting me to mount her doggy style, which is the only way horses can have sex. She says I would be a great sire and that she doesn't mind I am going through a phase. This was funny at first, but

---

* Marengo is perhaps trying to impress Copenhagen with his daring here. Horses can be extremely private about certain anatomical regions. For example, no horse would dream of allowing any but the most intimate of lovers to closely examine his hock.

she seems very certain. I mean really, very certain.[*]

And something else happened also. Thunderclap out of Stormfront by Death to the French, my old racing stablemate who used to tease me and who, at this distance, I think I can admit I had a little crush on, sent me a letter. He asked what his favourite regiments are doing – he is really nerdy for such a beta horse (beta, to repeat, being the first letter of the horse alphabet) – and then said, PS, he had sired three foals this year. I burst out crying. I had to pretend I had been stung by a giant bee.

I want a foal so something is left after me when I am inevitably blown up in this dumb war.[†] I finally understand why your Napoleon wants offspring. It is amazing that you have thought about foals also. It makes me feel less silly.

Oh, it's a few minutes later. I went into a daydream. In it, we were at Epsom watching the Derby, and the winner was Napoleon Bonaparte out of Marengo by Copenhagen. That can't happen of course. Can it? No, it can't. I know it can't. Stupid Copenhagen.[‡]

---

[*] This revelation casts radical new light on the later career of Eve's Apple. We all know she went on to become a fundamentalist preacher of the most terrible kind. Until the discovery of these letters, it was widely assumed that she was just a rotten apple. The knowledge that her later bigotry was born in disappointment and that she must have been very sad doesn't excuse the fact that she ruined thousands of horses' lives but at least you understand it a bit more.

[†] Copenhagen's feelings about offspring may have been influenced by his mother. See Appendix A.

[‡] A horse called Napoleon B out of Surrogate Mother

33

Because of the conversations with Eve's Apple out of Serpent by Normal is Best – I call them conversations but I didn't say much – I couldn't help myself imagining rude things about her, but they didn't arouse me. But then I thought that might be because I am in denial and how do you know if you're in denial because when you deny being in denial it is exactly what you would do if you were in denial? But then your letter arrived, and I knew again that it was a weird existential moment and I only like boy horses in that way.

Eve's Apple out of Serpent by Normal is Best read your letter because she is always going through my things. She went mental. She said you are perverting my natural desires, which are for her alone, only I don't realise. She is psycho.

Viscount Wellington is an earl now, and he won a battle at Salamanca the main thing about which was it was bloody hot, excuse my French. Is Russia hot? It will be with you in it.

Love,

Copenhagen

PS I want to say what you could do to me but I am worried about SOMEONE reading this.

∼

---

by Copenhagen Or Marengo won the Prix de l'Arc de Triomphe in 1841. It's not the same, but you've got to think it's interesting.

Dear Copenhagen,

I have encountered females like Eve's Apple before. They choose to believe what they wish to be true. So, Ms Apple, if you are reading this, take your mealy muzzle out of my lover's business. He is not for you. And if you persist in your harassment I will strike you with my cannon bone against your point of croup.

But dearest Copenhagen, there is no need to be ashamed of your yearning for offspring. It is only natural. And if you are spared a painful death in battle, you will no doubt be rewarded with many years at stud. Just do not expect to enjoy it very much.

But it is not merely for foals that you yearn. My years, though not so very great, have brought me some wisdom at least. You yearn for the contact of flank on stifle, and who can blame you? You are but a young horse, and it was your impetuousness and vivacious nature that first drew me to you.

What I am saying is this: I have had many adventures.[*]

---

[*] Marengo's only previous relationship was a perforce chaste long-term liaison with a piebald gelding called Vieu Flambeau. This brief correspondence between the horses, dated March 1810, was discovered taped over two cracked windowpanes in the Princess of Wales Conservatory, Kew Gardens:

Dear Vieu Flambeau,
I know I said that I would never write to you again, but I thought, as a courtesy, I should let you know that I have met someone else. You told me I would never meet another horse, because I am obsessed with my work and have no room in my life for love. Well, I am not and I do.

So many that I can't recall the specific details of any of them right now. You have yet to sow your wild oats. Therefore I say be free, Copenhagen, if it is really important to you, although some say that abstinence makes a horse better suited to battle, all the repressed energy, you know. Also I have invented a secret cypher for us to describe our imagined encounters and to keep them from prying eyes, Eve's Apple. It follows after my signature. To the casual reader it will appear merely as a decorative pattern of dots and dashes, but to us it will be filled with saucy meaning. I call it horse code.[*]

His name is Copenhagen. He is a racehorse and he is younger than you.
Please do not feel that you have to reply to this letter. I wish you well.
Kind regards,

Marengo

PS In the interest of scrupulous honesty, which was always more important to me than to you, I should probably say that I have not actually met Copenhagen. But we share a communion of the spirit, which is more than I ever had with you in fifteen years of eating out of the same manger.

And, dated three weeks later,

Dear Vieu Flambeau,
I have not received a reply to my last letter. Could I just check that I have the right address?
Best wishes,

Marengo

[*] A team of 119 cryptographers stationed at an anonymous

So you do not actually have to have real sex at all. But if you absolutely must, I release you from the bonds of fidelity, and don't give a moment's thought about how I might feel about it, all alone in Russia, where it is getting colder by the minute. Be free, Copenhagen, and do as you will; for though your body may be lent to another, your heart will remain mine.

Russia does not live up to my hopes, by the way. The weather is awful – constant bloody rain, I am at serious risk of hoof rot.* Napoleon is in a frolicksome mood, no doubt because he is away from the ball and chain. (Marie-Louise is the ball, because she is fat.) He whistles the Marseillaise incessantly and claims that we

---

business park just outside Uttoxeter spent seven and a half months in 2010 deciphering Marengo's horse code, eventually deducing that it is exactly the same as Morse code except with the H and the M transposed.

* Amateur hoofologist Luke O'Shea writes to us again:

> *From the portraits, Copenhagen and Marengo have beautiful lower legs and hoofs. What hoof care regimes do they follow?*

This is an enormous topic and one we cannot begin to go into here. We suggest that the interested reader sees *Horse Hoof Care* (2009) by Richard Kilmesh and Cherry Hill. *Knack Leg and Hoof Care for Horses, A Complete Illustrated Guide* (2008) by Micaela Myers and Kelly Meadows is another one, but not as good. For free thinkers, and there aren't enough of us, quite frankly, there is Joe and Kathleen Kamp's *Why Our Horses are Barefoot: Everything We Have Learnt About the Health and Happiness of the Hoof* (2011).

are winning. But this is mainly because the Russians are not turning up to the war, and I for one find this odd. We are lately arrived in Moscow to find it empty but for the faint aroma of vodka. Some of the other horses think the Muscovites have run away, but I am unsure.

Ah, it is unsettling, but for now we hold the capital, and one should not look a gift horse in the mouth. I will think of you and take courage.

Onwards!

Marengo

.... . .-.. .- .. —— / -. . . .-. -.. ...

～

Dearest Marengo,

That was a brilliant genius method for getting me the way to break the code without Eve's Apple seeing it. And what you wrote! It made me feel really hot under the martingale!

It is totally amazing that you want me to sow my wild oats. I thought that wasn't something you would like so I never even considered it, but after you said I should, I went straight away and found Mortar Wants a Pestle out of Confused by Something Has Always Seemed Wrong Somehow who has been looking at me all campaign in a way I don't think he understood. Now he does! He understands over and over again, actually. I am quite tired thinking about it. Since then, two days ago, I have also stood rut with Kilimanjaro

38

Rises Like Olympus out of Africa by Toto, who is not as impressive as he sounds, and Giant Tower out of Big Hammer by Never Says Stop, who is. Oh boy. And when I did that thing with my tail to Giant Tower, who has been campaigning for eight years and has a string of faithful mares somewhere in Lincolnshire and says what goes on war, stays on war, and any port in a storm of lead, he said I was the best he'd ever had and he'd reward me and he really did. Then there were some others but they were just quickies.

I thought the best bit would be describing it all to Eve's Apple. But she said it meant I didn't really love you, but was going through a phase like all the other warhorses, like Giant Tower. I said I wasn't. She said I was and she would show me something Giant Tower couldn't do. I am sorry, but I was so tired that I let her do it. She was right that it was different . . . in a gross way!! I do want foals, but if I have to do that then UGH!

On the subject of foals, Thunderclap sent me pictures of his eldest, who is called The Purpose of Life out of Any Old Mare by Thunderclap. He is soooo cute, and he really is his daddy's boy. He'll break some hearts when he's older, by which I mean next year.[*] I wonder if I'll meet him? It's funny to think he's much closer to my age than you are.

---

[*] The Purpose of Life out of Any Old Mare by Thunderclap went on to become a horse model, a favourite of the French inventor of photography Joseph Nicéphore Niépce because of his ability to stand very still and his lovely long eyelashes.

In the code, I will describe me doing to you what Giant Tower did to me.

I bite your withers in sexy adoration,

Copenhagen

- .... / .. ... / -. --- – / -- --- .-. .... / -.-. --- -.. .

~

Dear Copenhagen,

I am glad you have taken my advice. I am French, and we understand the passions and cravings of the body. There is no word for jealousy in our language, aside from '*jalousie*'. Even so, perhaps, in future, you will give me fewer details? And if, when describing your fantasies in code, you would not mention any other horses by name, or size, that would be my preference.

If there is a future. Oh much loved horse, I am in despair, I am even, I must admit it, terrified. Moscow is burnt to the ground and we are defeated. We retreat through the cold, oh it is so cold, Copenhagen – I fear my chestnuts will freeze off – chestnuts, as you know, being the small horn-like protuberances above a horses's knees. The Russians attack us at every turn. And every day more horses die. There is no grass beneath this wretched snow. As my Napoleon says, an army marches on its stomach, and that stomach is empty. But it is worse than that. I can barely bring myself to say it. The soldiers have no food. They are on the brink of starvation. And so . . . They are eating us, Copenhagen.* After so many

---

* Over 200,000 horses died during Napoleon's disastrous

40

years of service given selflessly by thousands of horses to this human war. There is no loyalty, only betrayal. Someone should write a play about this.

Copenhagen, I fear I will not make it home. I fear I will die without ever seeing your face.

Yours, always, whatever that may mean,

Marengo

∼

Dear Marengo,

Please say you are alive. I can't believe what I wrote. Please forgive me. Even if you do, I probably won't ever forgive myself. Even if you can't forgive me, please write back.

Please be alive, all my love, love, love, in haste, please be alive,

C

∼

And that is where the letters end. A note on the packet, however, suggests there may possibly be a further instalment stuffed into the lining of one of Copenhagen's old saddles at the National Tack Museum in Milton Keynes. We can but hope.

Russian campaign, many of whom were killed by soldiers for food. Some revisionist historians have suggested that this was not due to starvation, but because the French really like eating horses.

PACKET 3

THE NATIONAL TACK MUSEUM LETTERS

Good evening, fellow horsetorians. For some weeks, we have been following Napoleonic War paper trails in order to track down the extraordinary correspondence between the young, feisty Copenhagen and the wise, battle-worn Marengo, warhorses to Wellington and Bonaparte respectively. At the end of the last packet of letters, Copenhagen was in terror that his beloved had been lost on the bloody retreat from Moscow. This next instalment, discovered in the lining of one of Copenhagen's old saddles at the National Tack Museum in Milton Keynes, continues the story.

Dear Copenhagen,

I am alive. Or at least my body obstinately lives, and drags my soul with it. Oh, despair! The shoe of war is on the other hoof. Every day the glorious empire shrinks. Mr Napoleon, who once commanded such fear and respect, is an object of mockery. People make stupid remarks such as 'Where does Boney hide his armies? Up his sleevies!' This is what passes for humour in nations less comically enlightened than France.*

Although indeed, soon we will be able to fit the entire army inside Napoleon's battle-jerkin, which as you know is well-tailored but compact. We have lost so many soldiers fighting Russia that the Emperor has started recruiting old men and children to his side. These troops are known as the Marie Louises because, like Napoleon's wife, they are weak, irritating, and mostly to be found lying on their backs.

What is the point of me now? My life is my work, and you, of course, but you are so far away. It breaks my heart that you are on the wrong side of this war, and I fear that your youthful innocence will be corrupted by the evil one who rides upon you. By which I do not mean any particular equine companion with whom you are exercising your youthful vigour because as we have discussed I am completely and in every way fine with that. These horses you dally with are not very tall, are they? No, no, do not indulge me, it is merely the

---

* Nations less comically enlightened than France: none of them. Oh, maybe Peru.

insecurity of my broken spirit taking command of my words.

Ever yours,

Marengo

〜

Dear Boney M,

Thank the horsey god you are alive! But you sound really down in the dumps. Don't worry about losing. The main thing is that the war gets finished and so there is less chance of us dying in it.

I am really, really happy you are alive, and I have sent you a book called *Seven Habits of Highly Effective Warhorses*,* which I found super-helpful, especially chapter six, which is about visualisation techniques for not identifying too closely with bad decisions made by your rider.

Speaking of visualisation and being in the dumps, here's a tip straight from the horse's mouth, ha ha. In my old racing days, when I got glum, other horses said I was being haunted by the Black Dog. I was pretty scared by this and it made things much worse. I mean,

---

* *Seven Habits Etc.* was written by Pacifist out of White Feather by Surrender Monkey, whose weirdness is probably best explained by saying that his mother was English and his father was French. He went on to write a series of increasingly saccharine books of advice, culminating in the unreadable *Gee Yourself Up, Gee Gee*. How do we know it's unreadable? There's only one way to find out.

a Black Dog! But then I thought, what if the glumness is just a black FROG? Just a crappy frog! End of problem. I hope that helps*.

I am not going to be insensitive and talk about how badly the war is going for you, don't worry!

Lots of love,

C

~

Dear Copenhagen,

I would prefer it if you did not call me Boney M. I do not know why but I feel it lacks dignity. Also, please do not bang on about frogs. You are clearly implying that the French are unthreatening and crappy. Well, we are not.

Thank you for the book, I have already read it some time ago, which is why I am such an effective warhorse. I am sending you *Warhorses Are From Mars, Because Mars Is the God of War*, which is even better. Once you've read it, you will understand that sometimes I need to go into my cave, which is not literally a cave, but a mental cave. Although mine is not a cave, because I do not like caves. It is a mental gazebo.

There is no need for you to tip-hoof around my feelings regarding the war. It is not over until the fat mare whinnies.

Let the best horse win! (I am not saying that I am

---

* A black frog is worse than a black dog any day (I am scared of frogs).

the best horse, but I have been doing this a lot longer than you.)

Marengo

~

Dear M,

I am sorry for trying to be sensitive!

Frog can mean many things.* It can mean frog, or Frenchman, or a part of a horse's hoof, or a sort of hoarseness in the throat, which is not a horse reference incidentally. You are being pig-headed (which might be a pig reference, I am not sure.)

For your information, *Warhorses Are From Mars* is really quite discredited these days, in England, because of its assumption that we horses are at war, when we are not, it is just the humans.

I particularly don't like the chapter about how warhorses must not accept the possibility of losing. In my old racing days the first thing I learnt was that almost all horses in almost all races, are losing. You

---

* It really is surprising how many things frog can mean. As well as those listed by Copenhagen, it can also mean a type of belt loop, a variety of ornamental braid, part of a railroad track, the thingy you use for supporting stems in a flower arrangement, and the nut of a violin bow. (Violin bows have nuts. Copenhagen take note.) Somebody should invent some new words, in our opinion, before frog collapses under the strain.

have to be able to cope with it or you will go mental. I suppose you were brought up differently. I suppose we are very different horses.

Anyway, since you can handle it, Boney is not just being mauled by the Russian bear (grr). We are being very successful in the peninsula. If this is what the French army is like, I think you have been very lucky so far not to taste English backbone, which the French don't like up them. I don't quite understand what that means but the soldiers say it all the time. You say we are evil, but when we marched into Madrid, everyone was cheering us. It's hard to say we are the evil side when so many people want us to win.* The cheering was quite a head rush, actually.

Then we stormed Ciudad Rodrigo and captured the French army siege train, whatever that is, but it is apparently a good thing and Wellington was made a Spanish Duke.

Then we stormed Badajoz for weeks, and it was a nightmare basically. In English, the soldiers who have to charge into the breech, and who almost all die, are called the Forlorn Hope, which is very poetic, although Pedant out of Old Stager by Seen It All Before says it comes from the Dutch *verloren hoop* meaning lost heap

---

* Barely even know where to start with this one. Popularity of a movement does not guarantee lack of evilness, cf. Nazi Germany, slimline tonic water, etc. S.T.W., maddeningly, is packaged identically to normal tonic water, and the Kilburn High Road branches of Sainsbury's Local and Tesco Metro only stock slimline.

and as such is an example of false folk etymology.*
When we eventually did capture Badajoz, the soldiers
ran amok for two days, murdering and raping according
to the ancient military custom.

So, whatever Boney thinks, it turns out that

---

* Horses can be as pedantic as the next animal but Pedant
out of Old Stager by Seen It All Before seems to have been
a particular horror. The back of one envelope in this packet
of letters contains a long list of false folk etymologies in
Copenhagen's distinctive hoof, under the heading, 'Old
Stager Says . . .'

*1. 'Candelabra' does not actually derive from the custom
whereby prostitutes in eighteenth-century Vienna wore
a small lantern containing three lamps in their cleavage
to 'light the way home'. These lanterns were based on an
original design of Humphry Davy.*
*2. 'Gee Yourself Up' does not come from some shortening
of 'Gee Gee' and is nothing to do with horses at all. Except
that Gee Gee is an extension of Gee, because people told
horses to 'Gee Up!' and children heard and thought horses
were called 'gee gees', so it does have something to do with
the expression 'gee gee' but not in the way oh I am so bored
writing this down does any of it really matter I thought
it was interesting when Pedant was saying all these things
but I am just tired now and want some cobnuts and I am
only writing all this down to persuade him I am taking him
seriously.*
*3. I think if I put in another number he will think I am still
copying down what he says. His voice is putting me to sleep
now, basically.*
*4. I am bloody going to stop now, I mean what do I owe this
boring bloody horse. Right, this is it. Enough.*

Wellington is really good at this. In my old racing days, we'd have called him 'a duck', meaning something which looks a bit hopeless but which is actually WELL fast.

On the subject of my old racing days, Thunderclap out of Stormfront by Death to the French, who is the horrible racehorse I used to know who is obsessed by wars, sent me yet another message. He has really changed his tune. He has eight foals now and feels trapped by fatherhood, and asks me if I ever think back to my old racing days. He also asked for any news of the battles and especially of Robert Craufurd's Light Division, who are his favourite. It was my mournful duty to inform him that Black Bob Craufurd died at Ciudad Rodrigo. Craufurd was a noble comrade. *Ah, la guerre.*

I hope you are less grumpy.

Love,

C

~

Dear Copenhagen,

I am not 'grumpy'. Nor am I 'pig-headed'. I am facing the collapse of everything I believe in and have fought for in my fifteen years of partnership with the Emperor Napoleon Bonaparte. This is not a passing moment of petulance.

Before you go boasting about your Rodrigo and your Badajoz and the cheers of your Spaniards, remember that for some of us this is not a bit of Euro-tourism to pass the time now that we have taken early retirement from our less than glittering racing career. For some of us this is not just another game that will be rewarded with a silver cup, a rub-down and a nosebag of oats.* For some of us this is the battle between right and wrong. Look at the behaviour of your troops at Badajoz. You say I identify too much with my rider, perhaps you should identify a little more with yours.

And the Spanish that you revere so much are being completely unreasonable. Napoleon has come up with an excellent plan for peace wherein King Ferdinand the

---

* Horse fan Emma Southerington writes:

Dear Marengo Horse,
Oats for breakfast, lunch and supper must get rather dull after a short while; and, as you are such a wise, intelligent horse of abundant talents; I was hoping you might share your favourite French fancy oat-cuisine secrets?

Marengo replies:

Dear Ms Southerington,
On the contrary, I follow a macrobiotic diet, centring, as recommended for optimum health, on unprocessed, unrefined, ideally organic grains (thus, mais oui, *largely oats for breakfast, lunch and supper.) I also take good care to chew my food thoroughly before swallowing. I almost never get the colic.*
It may not be fancy, but look at all the rich food Monsieur Napoleon eats, and the terrible effect it has on his digestion. I should know, being in the firing line. (That is a little warhorse joke. It has a double meaning, do you see?)
I hope this helps.
Marengo

Seventh will be restored to his throne the moment he marries his niece Zénaïde,[*] who by all accounts is a lovely girl[†] of eleven. But he has refused. This is pernickety and absurd. If he were a horse this would be considered a match most prudent! But no, so more must die.

You will pardon me if I find it funny that you presume to lecture me on the loss of comrades under the present circumstances. Perhaps you would be better sharing your war stories with Thunderclap, who clearly understands nothing of the realities of combat, if the pair of you can obsess so mawkishly over the loss of one – one! – compatriot.

Marengo

PS That cannot be true about ducks. You must have misunderstood the meaning of the expression.

∿

Well, Marengo,

You say you are not grumpy. So you know, I was being kind. What you really are being is what we, in my old racing days, called a bad loser.

You talk of right and wrong, but still we are cheered all around Spain apart from Badajoz because of all the raping and murdering. Unlike your oppressive

---

[*] Zénaïde Bonaparte eventually married her cousin Charles at the age of twenty-one, a match first floated when she was five years old. They had twelve children.

[†] Not ALL accounts. Someone said she was a brat.

Bonaparte, we feed the locals and we pay them. It is practical and realistic, and perhaps, forgive me, they like that more than empty declarations of universal freedom and empty stomachs under the French jackboot.

We have suffered a terrible reverse at Burgos, which you were probably happy to hear and probably hoped I had even died, but no luck there for you.

I don't care who wins this stupid war, like I always try to tell you but you never bloody listen, but if I did care, then I could say England is about real things like loyalty, food on the table and paying your way, not ideals like freedom that don't do anyone any good.

I think I understand what you are going through and I am trying to be here for you, but you make it bloody hard. And you could try being supportive of me for a change. Thunderclap out of Stormfront writes to me every day. At least somebody appreciates what I am doing here.

Love, because I am loyal,

Copenhagen

PS It IS true about the ducks, actually. Of the ten fastest birds, six are types of duck, including the red-breasted merganser, the mallard and the common teal, and another one of the ten fastest birds is the spur-winged goose, and a goose is basically a fat sort of duck. Please do not belittle me if you can stop yourself for five minutes.

~

Dear Copenhagen,

You are being impish, presenting arguments in which you can hardly believe. It is Thunder-claptrap, turning your head. He has always envied me. You claim to be fighting for loyalty, food, and what was the other one? Pay as you go? But my Napoleon stands for liberty, equality and fraternity. If you oppose these things, you fight for servitude, inequality and the sisterhood, which is ridiculous. But perhaps you would genuinely rather live as a fat slave than die hungry but free. In which case, you disappoint me.

You say you care nothing of battles, so why do you document them exhaustively? You call me a bad loser, so why do you gloat when you win? Losing is bad when you fight for something you believe in, but I would not expect you to understand that. Your attempts to goad me by saying I wish for your death are beneath you – you know this cannot be true. Your attempts to make me jealous by talking of Thunderclap are pathetic. You know I am incapable of *jalousie*. As for your constant references to your old racing days, enough! In your old racing days you were a terrible racehorse!

But I forget that you are barely more than a child. Of course you are naive, of course you are bedazzled by the glamour of war, of course you are excited to win at something for the first time in your life. And let me tell you, all is not lost for the French! We may only have a handful of pathetic halfwits and doddering ancients on our side, but Napoleon has masterminded a series of such triumphs this week. The victory may yet be ours! And by some happenstance, at the very peak of our army's resurgence, it is the day of St Valentin. So I forgive you all your tactlessness. If only Wellington would concede defeat so that we could be reconciled. Fate may have put us on opposing sides, but my heart remains yours, always.

Marengo

PS Did Thunderclap send you a Valentine's card? I do not mind if he did*.

~

Dear Marengo,

I am happy that you are having a brief Indian summer of late-career success, but I don't need you to forgive me, thank you very much. You are not just a bad loser, you are also a smug winner.

And anyway, we have entered Toulouse, actually,

---

* People complain about the commercialisation of Valentine's Day. Horses do not have this problem because no money changes hoof. This is just one of the ways horses are better than people. It is said that any horse who pays to win love, which should be freely given, is reborn to eternal life as an equine statue, damned forevermore to absolute hunger and tiredness and frankly bored rigid. It's a horrible thought and it is why horses celebrate when they see an equine statue destroyed. No one knows what they think of that ginormous white horse that is being put up in Ebbsfleet. It will probably be used to give naughty foals nightmares. That's what it should be called, actually: The Nightmare of Kent.

so we are doing just fine, thank you. Wellington was incredibly stressed because he lost 4,568 men. Everyone knows that Napoleon doesn't care how many of his soldiers die. Forget the fancy words – who really cares about individuals? I'm just saying.

You are right. I don't care about the battles. But I listen to you about your stupid battles because I know you care. But the moment I start doing OK at battles you turn nasty, like you are threatened by my success or something.

We are falling out and I hate it. I don't want to fall out with you. You are the most amazing horse in the world and it breaks me up inside to think you are unhappy. I am interested in you when you are winning battles, and I am sad when all your friends are being eaten in Russia and so on, but we have to take this relationship to the next level. It cannot be totally dominated by whatever you happen to be feeling about your job.

I love you,

Copenhagen

PS I got several Valentine's cards, as it happens. Who knows who they were from?

~

Dear Copenhagen,

Napoleon has a saying: 'Do you know what is more hard to bear than the reverses of fortune? It is the baseness, the hideous ingratitude of man.' So it is with us, except that you should replace the word man with the word horse. Everything you have learned of the art of war you have learned from me, and now that you have taken all you need, you turn your famous bottom.

Your accusations are absurd. The idea that I might be threatened by your success! I cannot even begin to list the ways in which that is ridiculous, so I will not. Except to say that I am a horse of grandeur, and of dignity, and of experience, although I am not as old as some horses think, and I have faced down the canons of the enemy since before you were born, and I can face down the Wellington boot, even with your hoof in it.

You say that my work dominates everything, but you are wrong. I care for nothing but you, and the Napoleonic wars. These wars are bigger than you and me, and not because I am a small horse.

Napoleon has another saying: 'Courage is like love, it must have hope for nourishment.' Well, I have lost all hope. Although I still have courage, so perhaps that saying is not so relevant here.

But as you will have heard and no doubt celebrated, Napoleon has abdicated. What you may not know is that he then swallowed a concoction of opium, belladonna and white hellebore which he has worn in a phial around his neck ever since he was nearly captured by Cossacks near Moscow. He gave none to me. His plan was to leave me alone in this world. Luckily for France, it had gone off, so he merely threw it up again, but the fact remains, he, too, abandoned me.

And thus I must leave you. I cannot bear to continue this correspondence. You claimed to be a stayer, but you lied. This rupture has nothing to do with pride. You are young and have options who send you cards. Go to them.

Forlorn Hope,

Marengo

PS I have to concede you were right about the ducks.

And that's the last letter we've been able to find. Rumour reaches us, however, of a further packet lurking somewhere in an attic of military ephemera belonging to former Australian fast bowler Brett Lee.* We can but hope.

---

* Brett Lee's attic is a real cornucopia of delights. It is worth making friends with him and listening to all his Shane Warne stories just to spend half an hour picking through the Gatling guns (he hasn't even got a permit!).

Incidentally, one of the greatest greyhounds of all time is named after Brett Lee. In 2004 he was sold as a breeding dog for Aus\$800,000. He commands a stud fee of something like Aus\$10,000. It's not strictly relevant to the job in hand. Or is it? (It isn't.)

PACKET 4

THE BRETT LEE PAPERS

As you know, the BBC has been honoured to have the opportunity of putting before the public an extraordinary collection of love letters written between Wellington's great warhorse Copenhagen and his Napoleonic counterpart, Marengo. The previous set of letters saw Napoleon resign after his shattering defeat in Russia. Marengo was in despair. Copenhagen accused him of being too bound up in his work to commit to a serious relationship. Marengo, dejected, wrote that he felt unable to continue with the correspondence. This packet, discovered in an attic of military ephemera belonging to former Australian fast bowler Brett Lee, takes up the story where it left off . . .

Dear Marengo,

You said you didn't want to speak to me again, and I didn't reply. It was your responsibility if you wanted to change it.

But you did sound basically like you'd gone mental, and because I care about you – I bloody care, much thanks I get for it – all I am doing, *all I am doing*, is checking that you are all right. If you are all right, I'll never bother you again, because you are obviously on a much higher plane than me and emotions don't affect you. I'm only doing this because I thought there was something between us, even if you didn't.

And maybe you don't understand emotional honesty anyway, and so you need someone else to make the effort to break through your bloody intellectual reserve. So tell me you're all right, that's all I ask. I will always be your friend, whether you want me to or not.

Oh, by the way: you hinted that there might be something going on between me and Thunderclap out of Stormfront by Death to the French, my former tormentor and current, wannabe best friend, or between me and all the other horses I had sex with, but may I remind you 1) that Thunderclap has eight foals and 2) that you said you didn't mind me having sex with those other horses. I have stopped now anyway. I just stand around thinking of you. For some reason. I must be stupid.

In love, lightly crossed out so still clearly visible, in friendship.

Hoofprint,

Copenhagen

～

Dear Copenhagen,

What a curious English term it is, this 'all right',
when, in the words of your great philosopher Thomas
Hobbes,* life itself is nasty, brutish and short. (A
phrase which has also been unfairly used to describe
Mr Napoleon.) How can 'all' ever be right in this most
cruel of existences?

Thus no, I am not 'all right' – the years take their
toll on the heart as well as the hooves, although I have
some special unguent for the latter – but were you to
ask me in the French way, '*Ça va?*' – which means, in
your simple tongue, 'Does it go?' – I would answer yes,
it does still go, onwards ever onwards. As you are no
doubt aware, my beloved Napoleon is in exile on Elba,
and I am not. I am kept comfortable but alone in some

---

* The order in which horses rank human philosophers is:
5. St Augustine (because he is St Augustine of Hippo and
hippo means horse), 4. Locke (all horses realise that the
self is best defined through continuity of consciousness), 3.
Montaigne (they particularly admire his essay *On Warhorses*:
'I do not willingly alight when I am once on horseback, for it
is the place where, whether well or sick, I find myself most at
ease') 2. Jonathan Swift (because of the Houyhnhnms), and
1. Garamesh of Tir (Horses remember him, we don't. He
was the first person to tame horses and his great saying was,
'I bet tame horses will be really useful').

64

French backwater meadow, where the grass is sweet enough and the view tolerable, and I have a makeshift shelter of sorts for when the weather turns inclement. This is a time for reflection and self-scrutiny, and to my remorse I find that you were correct all along and I am a big enough horse to admit it, though I am technically only a pony. It has truly ever been all 'war, war, war' with me. Well, it is no more war, war, war! What is it good for, *hein*? Absolutely I do not know.

Late in life I am perforce discovering the way of the lie-in and the afternoon nap, and sometimes the morning nap and the evening nap as well. There is nothing else to do here but nap. It is all nap, nap, nap. Consequently, I am indolent and turning to fat. You would not recognise me. I fear you would even be ashamed of me.

I miss Napoleon with a pain that grips my entire body. Although that is not as much as I miss you, for that pain grips my entire soul. And it is I who am at fault for this. I thank you for reaching out the hoof of friendship, and know that I can dream of no more than that.

Tell me your news, dear Copenhagen.

Love, yes love,

Marengo

Dear Marengo,

Oh wow. I am so glad I wrote! That was a beautiful letter. Does this mean you want us to be, you know, again? I'm going to pretend it does because my whole body feels sort of light just thinking about it.

I'm glad you are having a rest at last, you totally deserve it! I knew it was only work that came between us. Do give this new life a chance. You might find it fun.

It is all go in Paris. Wellington has been made ambassador to France, which seems tactless. For his embassy, he has bought a massive hotel, which in this period means house rather than hotel. Everyone is falling over themselves to give the general presents. The king gave him two vases – big mistake, Wellington hates vases – and a tray which was originally painted for Napoleon's mother and which features Napoleon and his Mameluke slave hunting in funny hats. Why they thought Wellington would want a tray in general or this one in particular I do not know. Also, what is a Mameluke? It sounds like a sort of cat, but that cannot be the case.

The hotel used to belong to Napoleon's sister Pauline, who Wellington calls a heartless little devil. He has hung a quite revealing portrait of her in his room.[*] I wonder about his mental state, to be honest. He has hired Napoleon's cook even though he can't tell rancid butter from fresh and he has started sleeping with Napoleon's mistress, Josephina Grassini. You told me

---

[*] Pauline would have sat for a very revealing one, only the painter didn't realise.

she was annoying but I had no idea,[*] and Wellington is nuts about her.

Speaking of nuts, I have sent loads of messages to Thunderclap out of Stormfront by Death to the French asking him to get me some cobnuts, which I love and which you can't get here for some reason. I've asked him three times and he says he's looking, but nothing so far.

I'm actually quite bored. I think of you alone in a field quite a lot. Really quite a lot.

Love, again, difficult hoofprint in the shape of a heart,

Copenhagen

〜

Dearest Copenhagen,

I am humbled by your letter, that you would consider being, you know, with me again, after all that I have done. I do not know what it is that draws us together, but we appear bound, for good or ill. I, too, feel light.

As you know, I have no interest in gossip. Though I will say this: the behaviour of your Wellington seems

---

[*] This is tantalizing. We have no record of Marengo's views on Josephina Grassini one way or the other. This scrap of sentence hints at letters yet undiscovered. Grassini entered Napoleon's stable, as it were, at around the same time as Marengo, who may therefore have experienced some jealousy towards her, regardless of whether or not there is a word for that in French.

most bizarre to me. He has fought Napoleon with such bitterness, only now to strive to become just like him. Why does he not, as they say, go the full hog, and wear a bicorne hat and walk around with his hand shoved in his waistcoat? As for Josephina Grassini, if Wellington wishes her to return his affections I hope that he can afford it, as the last I heard her going rate was seventy thousand francs a year. And also, a guardsman's charger I know told me her lead carriage horse told him that he got totally exhausted with all her different night-time visits around Paris and also the suburban area.

Still no word from Napoleon on Elba. I suppose he has forgotten me. You know they have made him Emperor of that *deux-centime* piece of rock? It is plain stupid, and beneath his dignity to accept. I have produced dung heaps bigger than Elba, and I dare say more fragrant.[*]

I heard from Rover, an Elban carthorse who is a member of my book club,[†] that Napoleon, who has

---

[*] This viewpoint is expected from a metropolitan and sophisticated horse such as Marengo, but it is unfair on Elba. See *Isle of Splendour, Isle of Joy: A Carthorse's Perspective* by Rover. This book, much beloved of tourists, distils the hard-won reflections of a lifetime of dusty toil and is a paean to the harsh beauties of the bucolic way of life. Among Elba's many delights is Monte Capanne, at 1,019 m the 'roof of the Tuscan Archipelago' and if that isn't faint praise we don't know what is. There are two Elban rivers longer than 5 km, but one of them is not much longer and nor is the other.

[†] The internal politics of Marengo's book club are hinted at in this letter, discovered acting as lining paper in the

sock drawer of superstar of song and screen, Miss Barbra Streisand:

> *Dear Rover,*
> *You have asked me to write and apologise to the rest of the book club for the 'inappropriate vehemence' with which I expressed my opinion on Anna Sewell's novel* Black Beauty. *Very well, I apologise.*
>
> *Although I do not see what is inappropriate about my objections to the unseemly haste with which Captain, the retired warhorse in the novel, is replaced by the young pretender Hotspur after he is injured in the cab accident in chapter 44. If you would care to revisit the passage in question, I'm sure the reasons for my objections will be comprehensible to all. Captain, we recollect, is a 'fine old fellow' who has survived the loss of his master in the Charge of the Light Brigade – which I am assured will be one of the greatest tragedies (aside from the retreat from Moscow) that any army will ever see, once it happens. He has been reduced to pulling cabs, which, pace the feelings of our dear friend Big Yellow, is hardly a profession on a par with skilled battle-craft. But it would seem that robbing Captain of his dignity is not enough for Ms Sewell. For after that horrifying incident involving a brewer's dray, the unnecessarily graphic details of which I do not care to repeat, Captain's owner concludes:*
>
> *'He thought the kindest thing he could do for the fine old fellow would be to put a sure bullet through his head, and then he would never suffer more.'*
>
> *Perhaps this is true. I have seen many a comrade felled on the field of war rather than struggling on through terrible pain and mutilation. Oh! The look in those horses' eyes as they know the end has come! The grave welcome they give*

always hated riding, is out on horseback almost every day,[*] though whom he is riding Rover cannot say. He is myopic, although he is a great authority on Voltaire. I speak of Rover, not Napoleon.

Apparently, Napoleon's new horse looks quite sporty. It sounds to me like Napoleon is having some kind of crisis. Meanwhile I have not had anyone on my

---

that final blow! These are images I will never forget.

But then Ms Sewell continues:

'The day after this was decided Harry took me to the forge for some new shoes.'

Well. You will forgive me if this strikes me as cold.

In answer to your questions, I am not 'taking this too personally', nor do I 'need to move on.' Yes, I am aware that we read Black Beauty *four months ago and have since carried on to study* My Friend Flicka *(twee, forgettable),* The Horse Whisperer *(patronising, sentimental) and* Seabiscuit *(actually not bad, although it is a stupid name for a horse).*

Lastly, I am not 'sulking' because nobody voted for my suggestion. I am sure Mr Morpurgo will do fine without our custom. I was merely quiet that day because I ate some bad acorns.

No matter what you say, I am looking forward to our next meeting, where I will certainly 'shut up and let somebody else get a word in.' No doubt that 'somebody' will be you.

Your friend in literature,

Marengo

---

[*] This was probably an attempted cure for his haemorrhoids. It sounds like a bad idea, doesn't it?

back for months. This is not a euphemism. Though if it were a euphemism, it would still be accurate.

Tell me what is happening in Paris. I never thought I would miss the Tuileries, and, in fact, I don't.

Eternally yours,

Marengo

~

Dear M,

Don't worry about your Mr Napoleon. He is probably just so depressed that he will ride anything with hooves. It doesn't mean anything.

He can't be acting weirder than Wellington. I think they are both going crazy because they want closure, because they didn't get it in the war, because Napoleon threw in the towel without a final climactic battle. And now Wellington has won and Napoleon is in exile, and so they will never fight each other, so no closure for them.

Wellington worries me, actually. He isn't even speaking to his servants now. He communicates via little notes passed on by Holman, his valet. Holman, would you believe, looks like Napoleon.

I am surprised, given all the rest of it, that Wellington hasn't sent for you to ride. I made that as a joke, but now I think about it, I am literally surprised by this fact. That would be amazing, wouldn't it! We would both be here in gay Paree! It would be like a minibreak but we wouldn't have to go home. In fact, I've suddenly realised that must be what it is like for

71

Parisians all the time. Wow. They must be knackered.

Horses, horses everywhere, but they're mostly French and tetchy.

Love, nut-deprived hoofprint, they still haven't bloody arrived,

C

Dear Copenhagen,

Now you mention it, I too wonder why Wellington has not sent for me. Of course, I would sooner die than surrender. What humiliation it would be, to be paraded in chains through the streets of Paris, the crowd jeering and throwing ordures. But I would keep my head high, neither hearing nor seeing them, steadfast to the last. Afterwards, perhaps, a few loyal Republicans would risk their lives to rub salve where the chains had chafed. Brave Marengo, they would say, you will always be a hero to us. Yes, the more I think on it, the more it does seem like an oversight.

A gypsy horse came by my stable last night. Of course I set no store by hoofreading,* but she said

---

* Traditional gypsy hoofreading has a lot more in common with human Tarot than it does with palmistry. Each of the hooves represents one of four suits, which are named for parts of the bridle (Nosebands, Throat-lashes, Reins, Bits). Markings on parts of the hoof may represent pips or faces, each of which have meanings. The King of Bits represents the imminent arrival of a significant message, for example,

I had interesting fetlocks, so I let her have her way. She said she could see nothing in my future except for a love affair. I presume this means you. And she said that my war line has ended, and so the war in Europe is definitely over, so there will be no final climactic battle for any of us. I have finished that chapter in my book – literally; did I mention I have begun writing a memoir? Nothing significant yet, just a few preliminary scribbles about my life with the greatest general of the age. I can send you the first few hundred pages if you like.*

All of my worst fears have come to pass, and yet, *incroyablement*, life seems not so very bleak. I begin, I think, to enjoy retirement. With age comes resignation, perhaps, and putting these modest memories in writing helps.

But also, I have begun to receive letters from a most lively and intelligent horse, also late of the Napoleonic campaign, although in a far less prestigious role than mine. His name is Marseillaise but he likes to be called Marcy, and he is a handsome bay, standing seventeen

---

and the Eight of Reins an inconvenient change in the weather. Marengo's interrupted war line would be indicated by a cluster of low pips on the Throat-lash hoof (left fore).

* No trace of Marengo's memoir has been found, although there is a hint that it may have survived at least until the early twentieth century, as it is recorded that a First World War Belgian pack mule called Suchet died of deep vein thrombosis in all four legs after trying to read the whole of an unnamed Napoleonic horse's autobiography in one go.

hands and two inches high, taller I think even than you, Copenhagen!*

He is a most interesting fellow. We have a true companionship of the mind and we discuss ideas intensely, sometimes sending several letters a day. He is tormented by the notion that there is no such thing as a *bellum iustum* (which I do not need to translate for you as a just war) and for all that I quote him the relevant passages of Cicero and Aquinas, he says that any notion of just war is relativistic and contradicts theories of universal philosophy.

But I do not wish to bore you. How goes the search for your nuts? It saddens me to think of you without your favourite delicacy to amuse you.

Please write again soon,

Marengo

∽

Dear Marengo,

Thank you for your letter, it really cheered me up, especially the bit about my nuts. I'm really stressed about them. They remind me of Kent where I grew up and they are the only thing which keeps my coat in decent condition. It's the selenium.

Of course, I wouldn't dream of passing on gossip, because you are so above it, so I won't tell you that now

---

* Copenhagen might have liked to give Marengo the impression that he was a tall horse, but he was in fact only 15 hands high, barely more than a pony himself.

Wellington is sleeping with Napoleon's other mistress Mademoiselle George. She is a bit more of a slapper, and she said within earshot of her second-favourite afternoon trotting hack that Wellington was '*beaucoup le plus fort*' whatever that means.

I am glad that you have a new pen friend. He does sound like everything you might want in a friend. You probably don't even need me now! Joke. There are lots of horses here but I am quite lonely.

Love,

Copenhagen

～

Dear Copenhagen,

It is not 'gossip' if one is merely discussing facts which are true. I am not familiar with the term 'slapper' but I can imagine its meaning, if it means the kind of female who would react with enthusiasm and not revulsion when a man – Mr Napoleon, say – puts forty thousand francs down the front of her bodice.[*] Also, you asked me for the translation of '*beaucoup le plus fort*' – *fort* can mean stronger or louder, and so I conclude that in the context of lovemaking, Wellington makes a lot of pointless noise.

Your letter reaches me most elated. I never dreamed I would enjoy retirement so much. I feel like a much younger horse – what a shame you are so far away! That is just my little joke. But I was surprised to detect

---

[*] It was a special sort of bodice.

a note of jealousy in what you say about Marcy. Please put your fears at rest. After all, I have never been jealous of your many companions, and was it not you yourself who encouraged me to make a new friend? I promise you, what passes between Marcy and myself is purely platonic. Indeed we are both great admirers of Plato. Sometimes Marcy teases me by calling me Aristophanes, because I am prone to hiccups! How you would laugh if you were here. And imagine this! Marcy is being transferred to my field! It is completely coincidental, the stable in which he was living burned down. He was the only survivor, poor horse. I cannot wait for him to arrive.

In the meantime I am transfixed by the quest for your elusive nuts. Have they reached La Manche yet? (I cannot bring myself to defile that beautiful strip of water with the name 'English Channel'.)

With love, and reassurances,

Marengo

~

Dear Marengo,

READ THIS LETTER ALONE!

I promise you I am not being jealous and paranoid but I have asked every horse in Paris what Marcy is like. When I asked Escargot out of Garlic Butter by Crusty Artisinal Baguette, he totally wigged out. Apparently, Escargot was the horse originally chosen to join you in your field, but the night before he was mysteriously kicked in the fetlock by a very tall bay horse in a mask. The next day, all his potential replacements apart from Marcy were killed in a mysterious fire!

And listen to this: according to Escargot, Marcy's last two lovers were Toreador, an anonymous sort of horse Napoleon used for parades when he was stuck in Madrid for a few weeks once, and Herodot, the famous stud stallion from Ivenack, who Napoleon sent a squadron of soldiers to capture while he occupied Mecklenburg.* Can you see a pattern? Those other two horses are now dead.

I am going crazy with worry. I am going to find a way to get out there to protect you, even though apparently my cobnuts are finally on their way. Cobnuts are amazing.

I am coming, somehow,

Hasty hoofprint,

Copenhagen

~

COPENHAGEN STOP MARENGO HERE STOP EXCEPT NOT HERE STOP HOLD YOUR HORSES STOP MARCY HAS ARRIVED AND WE ARE ON THE MOVE STOP DO NOT COME REPEAT DO NOT COME STOP YOU MAY BE KILLED STOP NOT BY MARCY HE IS GREAT STOP BUT BY NAPOLEON EXCLAMATION MARK HE HAS ESCAPED FROM ELBA ANOTHER EXCLAMATION MARK THE WAR IS BACK ON THIRD EXCLAMATION

---

* It is said that all horses have a bit of Herodot in them. This is pretty much true.

WARHORSES OF LETTERS

MARK I SUPPOSE THE MORAL OF THIS STORY
IS NEVER LISTEN TO GYPSY HORSES STOP NEW
PARAGRAPH ANY NEWS OF YOUR NUTS QUESTION
MARK *JE T* APOSTROPHE *AIME* STOP MARENGO[*]

~

And there the letters end. It is rumoured that there are other packets in the private collection of a Danish chewing gum magnate, secreted into the velvet backing behind the fish knives of the Officers' Second Best Dining Service of the Coldstream Guards[†] and in various other places, but until new funding is secured from the Comedy Commissioning Department at Radio 4, who are practically the only people still financing original historical research, it is impossible to take this further. Maybe that funding will eventually emerge. We can but hope.

---

[*] Funnyman Scott Newnham asks, 'Will Marengo and Copenhagen ever meet and ask each other why the long face?' We would like to know this ourselves. In the meantime, Marengo comments, 'I do not understand this question. All horses have long faces. Mine is actually quite average.'

[†] For some reason people always buy sets of fish knives on *Bargain Hunt*, as if they have never watched the programme and therefore don't know that no one wants to buy fish knives. It drives us crazy. The only worse thing is when people buy those little nursery chairs.

APPENDIX A

These letters were sent to us by an anonymous Latvian. Why would an anonymous Latvian send them to us? We don't know.

Dear Copenhagen,

It is Lady Catherine out of whom you are out of, i.e. your mother. It is some time since we spoke, but I bumped into John Bull, by whom you are by, i.e. your father, the other day and he mentioned that he has three thousand foals.

I have only eight, things being what they are, biologically.

You are now two and I think it is time to consider The Future. I have asked around, and I do not think anyone could accuse me of interfering when I say that there are several extremely nice fillies and mares in your regiment. Eugenica out of Mad Scientist by

Professor Brainiac is the child of two doctors, and Red Tape out of Brief Encounter by Billable Hours is from a legal family. Horse law is unbelievably complicated.

Anyway, those are just two of your many options. Dreaming of the clip-clop of tiny hooves!

*Lady Catherine (Mum)**

~

Dear Mum (Lady Catherine),

It was very nice to hear from you after all these years (two). I am very well thank you.

It is also very kind of you to tell me about Eugenica and Red Tape. I am sure they are very nice fillies. I cannot promise that anything will happen with either of them but please do not think there is a suspicious reason for this. The reason is not suspicious, it's just that I cannot think of what it is exactly and I am very busy with learning how to be a warhorse. Some guy is constantly creeping up next to me and shooting a gun to see if I jump. It's really irritating.

I have a question. What would you think if I were to fall in love with a French horse. I'm just joking,

---

* Canadian archivomaniac Nancy Johnston writes: 'I understand from archival sources online that Marengo was born in Egypt and lived there until he was six years old. Have you discovered any correspondence, translated from Arabic, from Marengo to his family, his sire or mare, back in Egypt? Does he describe those early years or is it wrapped in mystery?' Wrapped in mystery. For now.

obviously, but what would you feel about it, really? Even though it is a joke?

Also, can I just check that the main thing you want is for me to be happy and that foals are just an extension of that, not the be all and end all? I am sure that must be it, but I am just checking.

Love.

Copenhagen

∾

Dear Copenhagen,

What an amusing horse you are!

I particularly enjoyed your joke about fancying a French horse. We both know it would kill me if that happened and your dear father too, who I got to know very well indeed during the fifteen minutes we were together and then the five minutes we saw each other for the other week. After all, his name is John Bull! Anyway, everyone knows that French horses are all trollops who will stop at nothing and they SAY they eat nothing but chestnuts and cream all day it is just a miracle about their size zero withers, but we all know that behind all their stalls it STINKS of SICK. Also, it is very funny what you say about foals. OF COURSE it is only foals that count. That is what sexual attraction is for. The rutting is marvellous and you can't help yourself and you feel like a real horse for the first time in your life, but for companionship and conversation, you will probably be just as well with horses of your own sex even. You will learn this when you are older and less randy.

Beget, beget, beget,

Mum

〜

Dear Mum,

I am not saying that I fancy a French horse, but I worry that some of the things you said about French horses might have accidentally made you appear as if you are a terrible old bigot. For a first thing, horses literally cannot vomit, so the thing you said about French horses doing that to stay thin is not true. In fact, French horses have real trouble with their weight sometimes, which just goes to show how much you know, and I don't mind if they are a little cuddly anyway, which goes to show how much you know about that as well. Not that it is relevant in this case, anyway.

I am not being disrespectful to point the above things out, just saying that it is not cool to be a bigot about race. Or anything else. I am sure that you are a tolerant horse deep down, aren't you?

I must go now because we are in the Peninsular and I have to carry Wellington to some or other battle as usual.

Dutifully yours,

Copenhagen

〜

Dear Copenhagen (Wellington's horse),

I've never written a letter like this before. You probably get hundreds of them and this one might never arrive anyway, because of the wars smiley face, but I would never forgive myself if I didn't send it and so here it is. I have seen pictures of you. You are not literally an oil painting but you are literally a sketch in various penny papers and that's not nothing.* I don't know how you could look so amazing with that beaky Wellington on your back.

My name is Ballerina out of Beautiful Deb by Lord of the Manor. As you may remember, Beautiful Deb is your aunt and she has been talking with your dam, Lady Catherine.

I know, I know! Mothers can be so annoying, and I suppose by following this up, I am being annoying too! Please forgive me, I am not normally like this, I promise!

Anyway, Lady C says that you are shy and are having trouble meeting the right filly. I am shy too! I am the favoured riding hack of Amelia, the second wife of Baron Tightgrumble, who is a parvenu who made a fortune out of jute and who is thirty years too early to be the antagonist in a Dickens novel, but you get the

---

* Art-hater Victoria Parkinson comments, 'Writing whole letters definitely puts the horses who can paint pictures to shame.' In fact, Marengo fancied himself a rather proficient dauber. Early in their relationship, he sent Copenhagen a portrait, saying, 'Now you too are literally an oil painting.' Copenhagen begged to differ.

idea. Lady Tightgrumble is much younger and very beautiful.

Well, I have probably gone on long enough, and I am sure you are very busy with the war. Don't worry that you are shy. Shy horses of the world unite, I say!

Tentatively!

Ballerina

~

Dear Ballerina,

Thank you for your nice letter. You have nice hoof-writing. What you said about looking nice was very nice. It was nice to get your letter.

I think the first thing to say is that you are right that our dams are annoying. The second thing is that my mother doesn't know me as well as she thinks she knows me. I don't mean anything rude when I say this, but we are almost certainly not as made for each other as she thinks.

Thank you for your nice regard,

Copenhagen

~

Dear Copenhagen,

Thank you for your fast and kind reply.

I completely understand. No problem. I will understand if you don't even reply to this. I just wanted to say that I am also not what my dam thinks!

In fact, I feel embarrassed that I let myself write to you pretending to be that quiet, shy horse. I suppose it is because, well, I think probably it is that I am incredibly bored here in the country and was trying to be the horse I thought you might want me to be.

Amelia Tightgrumble frequently talks to me about this subject. She says that Lord Tightgrumble has imprisoned her like a pretty songbird, that she is fenced away from society with nothing to employ her, nothing to strive for. She says that some day the dam will break and the earth will be stained with the blood of men like her husband (she means the kind of dam which holds back a river not the kind which begets a foal).

I totally connect with this. I am not a show pony, but I am stuck here with no outlet for my energy, no outlet of any kind. My only fellow equine is an ancient Shire horse with a rural accent so thick it took me months to realise he is a bit dim and only ever talks about wurzels and prize fighting.

I am in the prime of my life! I feel almost ashamed to admit it, but sometimes when my mistress is riding on me, I let my mind wander and imagine the thudding weight is a different kind of thing altogether. Often I emerge from my reverie to hear her giving little moans and yelps which I take to mean she has noticed my inattention and is irritated.

So, let us start our correspondence again, shall we, as two less orthodox horses than our dams imagine, and let us see where that takes us. I will begin:

My name is Ballerina, and I believe in the rights of

the individual horse. I believe that however much we are bred to the bridle, our minds must always be free. Under the name 'Free Radical' I contribute regular pieces on the use of violence (read 'Buck up!') to *I am an Animal*. I am also standing for local elections as a libertarian anarchist.

Relieved to be writing like a grown-up,

Ballerina

~

Dear Ballerina,

That was a very interesting letter. I think that you sound super, but— What I mean is, now that I know that you are not shy and everything, and you are a modern filly (or is mare the more appropriate term?) I can explain honestly what I meant when I said my dam doesn't really know me.

I am sorry to say that I am a gay horse. Well, I am not sorry, it is bloody brilliant, but I hope you don't feel that I was a horse's arse for not saying this straight away. It's just that it is easier for me if my dam does not find out!

On the subject of animal rights, I am forward thinking, because I am gay. I will understand if you do not want to write back to me now, but if you do, I will happily continue with this correspondence.

I like the way you write to me as if I am an intellectual equal. Some horses, however much I love them, do not.

Best regard, firm hoofprint,

Copenhagen

~

Dear Copenhagen,

I am proud that you chose to come out to me! What I have to say to you is this: YOU MUST BE PROUD TOO! Do not be scared of telling your mother, even though my mum says she is a terrible nightmare. It's not as if you will probably ever see her again, even if you do not get hit by a cannonball.

I would be extremely happy to be your friend.

In friendship,

Ballerina

~

Dear Ballerina,

You're bloody right! I'll bloody tell her. Straightforward, clear, grasp the nettle!

Thank you,

Copenhagen

~

Dear Mum,

I have something extremely important to tell you, and I must do it as clearly as I can.

Imagine there is a squirrel called Berlin and he –

No. Take that back, imagine a pony called Oslo. Have you done that? He is just any old pony, except he's not that old, he's young and he's very big for a pony. OK, a horse called Oslo. This is just a story remember.

Now imagine that— Wait, you have registered that this horse is male? That is important.

Right – Oh, I keep saying 'he' so you knew it was male. He was male. I am getting in a muddle. Let's start again.

Imagine a ~~squirrel~~ horse called Oslo (male). He is going for a walk. He is in a field full of other ~~squirrels~~ horses of all different shapes, sizes and genders. He is thinking which of these horses he would like to be with for a chat and to share his nuts with.

He meets a ~~squirrel bloody hell horse oh my horsey god~~ mare called Pear of Dawn who comes over to talk to him and keeps nibbling at his hocks. He finds he does not want to share his nuts with her. Even when a very nice ~~squi~~ filly called Dancer comes over to him because her mother tells her to, it just ends up that Dancer and Oslo become best friends not nut-sharers.

Then Oslo meets, quite by chance, a ~~horse pony squirrel~~ pony called À la King and deep in his soul he feels that this horse is his soul mate.

Do you understand now?

Your affectionate son,

Oslo Copenhagen

❧

Copenhagen,

'*À la King*'!! Are you saying you have fallen in love with a French horse? I knew it! I wish you were gay!

In horror,

Mum

～

Dear Mum,

Sorry, I see that I forgot to mention that À la King was a male horse. That was the point of the story and I missed it out because I got muddled.

Gaily (hint),

Copenhagen

～

Dear Copenhagen,

My lovely boy, I understand. Probably two hundred of John Bull's three thousand foals are openly gay so this is hardly a surprise to me. I am just glad about the other thing. If you were in love with a French horse I would go berserk. They are enemy barbarians and they smell of garlic and I hate them and everything about them. The thought of you and a French horse made me want to vomit which, as you correctly pointed out, horses can't do.

I don't mind about the foals, not really. They were only an excuse for making contact after so long. The main reason was that I was bursting with pride that you had become not just a warhorse but our main warhorse in this war to end wars against the disgusting, horrible French. Though you could maybe stand at stud just a few times, just to make me happy if you care about that. No pressure. Just so there will be more future warhorses to fight against the horrible French, hopeful wink.

Love,

Mum

～

Dear Ballerina,

I have told my mother I am gay. I didn't tell her – I told her I was gay. Let's just leave it at that.

Copenhagen

～

BIBLIOGRAPHICAL ESSAY

The criminal (dare we say racist) neglect of non-human actors across almost every historical context is only slowly being addressed by the present generation of academics. Archives such as the British Museum's Fort William warehouse complex, The Smithsonian's Library of Uncatalogued Animal Materials (colloquially 'Animal Farm') and the Tashkent Bureau of Industry's Avian Literature Depository are obvious places to start, but they are only the tip of the horseberg. We recommend *Where the Wild Things Are: A Guide to Global Archives for the Bestially Inclined* (2004) by S. R. Stares as a sensible place to start.

Packet One

With respect to Copenhagen's first contact with Marengo, and Thunderclap's subsequent correspondence with Copenhagen, we drew heavily for further understanding on S. R. Stares's definitive *Battlemaniacs: Horses, War and Fan Culture* (2007). A precis of the book's main argument is published as 'Bloody Hell: Worshipping Warhorses' in *Loaded* magazine, June 2005. The 'man' part of 'Battlemaniacs' is a pun on 'mane'. Say it out loud if you didn't get it.

If you want to know all about the ancestry of racehorses, and some people do though we really don't know why, you should probably read the horse ancestry pages of *Who's Who*, which publishes them for Who's Who knows what reason. They are incredibly boring. It's just the same few sires and dams over and over again and by the end you're surprised that most of these horses don't have five legs.

With respect to Marengo's frequent and subtle wordplay, and his submerged references to the classics of equine literature ('The pasture of fame is a lonely one' and so on), we can make no more sensible recommendation than that you dive in at the deep end and immerse yourself in the plays of Horsey McGorsey, particularly the comedies (we have a soft spot for *The Mare Whom Loved a Sailor* but everyone has his or her favourite), in Red Mountain's *Lessons and Fables* and in the epic poetry of the Mongolian School. If you don't do this, you will never understand the half of what is going on. If you need a hand-holding overview, we recommend *By Horses, for Everyone: An Equine Literature Primer* (2001) by S. R. Stares.

Napoleon really did shoot out Masséna's eye. As S. R. Stares explains in 'Kingdom of the Blind:

Cyclopian Generals Through the Ages,' in the spring 2000 issue of *Monocle*, he was not the first and nor will he be the last. It is curious that Marengo never mentions Marshall Kutuzov, the one-eyed defender of Moscow against Napoleon. Possibly it is because Marengo was rather 'one-eyed' in his view of the war. For more on this particular metaphor, and on the comparative psychologies of monocularity and binocularity, consider 'Window to the Soul, How the World Sees the One-Eyed Man and How the One-Eyed Man Sees it Back' (S. R. Stares, *Punch*, 15 January, 1994).

Packet Two

On the training of warhorses, no library is incomplete without not having Dr S. R. Stares's incredibly boring overview *On the Training of Warhorses* (1987). However much you think you are interested in the subject, you are not interested enough in it to read this book.

On the tactics of Wellington, every English school-girl has giggled her way through *He's Behind You! Wellington and 101 Uses for Ridges (or One Use 101 Times!)* (S. R. Stares, 1982). The great bit is that the French NEVER realise, even when behind the ridge is the only place an army could be, unless someone had turned up to fight without an army, which Wellington never did. People are always trying to change things for the sake of it. Wellington wasn't like that. If something worked, he carried on doing it until someone caught on. No one ever did.

There is nothing new under the sun, and horses have been writing dirty letters to each other since Bucephalus, if not before. There are dozens of collections of these, none of which your mother would want you to read, which is why you probably already have. More interesting than any of the actual rude letters is S. R. Stares's incisive essay 'The Horse Has Bolted: Democratising Equine Pan-Sexuality', first published as part of *Unmuzzled: Subversion and Perversion Beneath the Saddle* (1988, ed. S. R. Stares et al). Under no circumstances read *Ride Me, Cowboy* (1999) a one-off experiment from Mills & Boon. The author, S. R. Stares, must have been drunk.

The psychology of foaling is little understood, but horses have always had foals so they must see something in it. In 'Spock and the Horse: the Great Foalcare Debate' in *Pony* (Autumn, 1990), S. R. Stares makes a brave attempt to understand the issue, but she doesn't really.

Many have wondered how the French soldiers made their knackered old steeds palatable on the tundra. The French have a way about them. All we know about the subject we learnt from *I Could Eat a Horse: History, Culture and Recipes* (S. R. Stares, 1987). In it, Stares points out that there is no intrinsic difference between eating horses and eating pigs, cows and so on. She is right. They are all murder.

Packet Three

Marengo's first letter in this packet drives at the heart of one of the most vexed of all animalological issues: do animals tell jokes? In *I Laughed Myself Horse: A Comprehensive Lexicon of Cavalry Puns and Wordplay* (1990) S. R. Stares is very unclear on the issue. It's not a good book but it's the best there is, and it's a good size for eating your supper off in front of the telly.

The black dog image is unpacked with supreme clarity by S. R. Stares in 'Don't Blame Me! The Appalling History of an Appalling Image' (*Puppies and Puppymen*, January 2004), for which the author was awarded the Prix Goncourt and the Freedom of the Canary Islands. A broader analysis of animals appearing in human images will shortly appear in *Happy as a Lark, Fat as a Puffin: Why Some Bestial Images Persist Where Others are Lost* (S. R. Stares, 2012). We thank the author for sending us an uncorrected proof of this work. It's absolutely hilarious.

On the subject of Black Bob Craufurd, if we can be excused the digression, we feel we simply must recommend *Black Bob Craufurd: The Life of Black Bob Craufurd*. This epic tome, published in three volumes last year, is the life's work of S. R. Stares and marks the triumphant culmination of thirty painstaking years of archival research. It transforms absolutely everything you think about Craufurd, in the likely event that you start off not knowing anything about him. You certainly don't end up that way.

The debate between Marengo and Copenhagen

with respect to French idealism and Anglo-Saxon pragmatism recapitulates the endless haggling of those torn between the continental and analytical schools of philosophy. It's hard stuff to get your head around but it's worth trying, if only so that you can get in with the Melvyn Braggs of this world. *The Total Moron's Guide to Talking about the Continental–Analytic Split for Time-Poor Dinner Party Guests* (S. R. Stares, 2000) is incredibly reductive but it will give you a veneer of learning and if you think anybody has much more than that you are sorely mistaken. Even Melvyn Bragg.

Copenhagen accidentally wanders into one of the thorniest minefields in nineteenth century battleology, and maybe in all battleology, when he blithely repeats the old myth that Wellington lost 4,568 lives entering Toulouse. This figure, of course, only refers to dead soldiers. To be fair, Copenhagen says 'men' where Wellington in his diary wrote 'lives' but even then this is to denigrate the several hundred additional male camp followers – blacksmiths, servants, pastry chefs and so on – who were killed. And when one thinks of Wellington's 'lives' one's heart rages at the thought of the tens of thousands of seamstresses, laundry maids, prostitutes, horses, chickens, sheep, pigs and others who breathed their last during that fateful week. Almost any conflict, we suppose, tells this same story, but the Toulouse campaign is the setting for *4,568 Be Damned*, probably the most minutely-observed and heartbreaking of all Segolene the Cat's many novels.

Buy the 1994 Penguin Classic edition, published by real penguins, with an introduction by S. R. Stares.

Packet Four

Copenhagen's concern for his lover's mental state was very reasonable, under the circumstances. In 'After the War is Over: Stress and Other Post-Conflict Issues as they Pertain to Retired Warhorses' (*Annals of Animal Psychology*, Autumn 2007) S. R. Stares presents compelling evidence that 80 per cent of all nineteenth-century warhorses suffered some form of mental change after leaving active duty, usually euphoria at not being shot at.

Copenhagen and Marengo both misunderstand the vicious interplay of gift and counter-gift which followed Wellington's 'tactless' appointment as ambassador to France. This was a calculated insult, as were the gifts with which the French responded. They knew very well that Wellington hated vases. This celebrated passage of passive-aggressive diplomacy was described by S. R. Stares in 'Another Bloody Vase: Calculating Insults in the Post-Napoleonic Context', which is the only chapter worth reading in *The Symbology of Offensive Present-Giving* (2006, ed. S. R. Stares). Robert should know, he got the book from his girlfriend last Christmas. Ex-girlfriend.

Of the later career of Holman, Wellington's valet, too much is known if anything. Once he realised that he had been hired on the basis of his physical resemblance to the French Emperor, he left service and started hiring himself out at parties. On seeing him at the Marquess of Cranberry Ball in early 1816, several society ladies fainted clean away from shock. The Cranberry Ball was very saucy and Holman was naked, which might have had something to do with it. Holman later formed an agency, Holman's, which still hires out lookalikes to idiots. His story was told in the 1996 National Theatre production *I am not Napoleon*, for which the author, S. R. Stares, won an Olivier Award.

With respect to Marengo's autobiography (still undiscovered), we are sorry to say that all equine memoirs are too long. They don't know what to leave out. If you want to see what we mean, read the personal story of Caligula's horse, Incitatus, in *The Day I Became a God* (1997, part of series 'From the Horse's Mouth', general editor S. R. Stares). He forgets that, in the end, no one is really that interested.

Marseilleise or 'Marcy' has caused us enormous headaches. No horse of that name appears in the official record. From the information collected by Copenhagen, we are tentatively willing to suggest, finally, that he might be the almost mythical 'Tack the Nipper', who left such a trail of destruction in Napoleonic stables between 1810 and 1815. The endless stream of books by half-baked Nipperologists is enough to make you want to run for the hills, and we know that raising this issue will overshadow every other scholarly claim we have made, but 'Marcy' was in the right places at the right times; he was clearly unstable; and he appears to have been conveniently close to an unfortunate number of 'accidents'. As to his real name, we cannot be completely certain. We prefer to agree with the doyenne of Nipperologists, S. R. Stares, who remarked at the end of *Chasing Shadows, a Nipperological Life* (2010) that the Nipper was 'just some horse. Does it really matter which one?'

ACKNOWLEDGEMENTS

This book would not have existed without the BBC Radio 4 series of the same name. Huge thanks to our producer Gareth Edwards, director Steven Canny, production team Jill Abram, Lucy Meggeson and Toby Tilling, and of course the brilliant actors who brought the story to life: Stephen Fry, Daniel Rigby and Tamsin Greig.

Special thanks also to the on-stage Copenhagens John Finnemore and Benet Brandreth, as well as all at Tall Tales and the Good Ship in Kilburn, where *Warhorses of Letters* was first performed. (Robbie was Marengo.)

In researching Copenhagen and Marengo's story we leaned heavily on *Wellington and Napoleon* by Andrew Roberts and *Marengo: The Myth of Napoleon's Horse* by Jill Hamilton, not to mention everything that comes up when you do a search for the word 'Horse' in the British Library. We'd also like to thank Wikipedia and everybody on the Internet.

ACKNOWLEDGEMENTS

It's been fantastic being part of the birth of Unbound. Thanks to everyone there, especially John Mitchinson, Dan Kieran, Xander Cansell and Justin Pollard, and Matt Railton at Colman Getty.

As ever, thanks to our agents: David Godwin and the DGA team, and Louise Greenberg.

And finally, thanks and apologies to our families and friends who have had to put up with a lot of bad horse puns.

SUBSCRIBERS

Mat Ablewhite
Denise Albury
Naomi Alderman
John Allum
Simon Amos
Lesley Kay Ansari
Nadia Erin Ansari
Sophia Parvin Ansari
Helen Arney
Jane Arundel
Charlotte Austin
Nicki Averill
Jarrad Ayling
Karen Banno
David Barke
Cynthia Barlow Marrs
Cat Barton
Andrew Baxter

SUBSCRIBERS

Kenny Beer
Caroline Beven
Liz Bickerdike
Amanda Borton
Audrey Bowden
Corrina Bower
Adc Bradley
Karen Bradshaw
Benet Brandreth
Jutta Brendemuehl
Nikki Brennan
Lesley Brinklow
Astra Bryant
Clifford Bryant
Elizabeth Bullock
David Callier
Lisa Campbell
Helen Campbell-Woodrup
Sheila Cannon
Jill Cansell
Xander Cansell
Ann Carman
Alison Carpenter
Will Chew
Nick Chouksey
Laura Clark
Martin Clarke
Ady Coles
Lisa Pearce Collins
Sophia Connor

A. J. Almeida Freixieiro
James French
Marc Fresko
Angelina Fryer
Vivien Gardner
Lucy Gaunt
Sophie Goldsworthy
Jo Gostling
Neil Graham
Lesley Grant
John Joseph Henry Green
Louise Greenberg
Mike Griffiths
Jean Gunstone
Daniel Hallifield
Friederike Hamann
Pernille Sybrandt Hansen
Deb Harrington
Jenny Harris
Shelley Harris
Graham Hassell
Dave Hawkins
Tory Heazell
Joanna Hepworth
Catherine Heywood
Bina & Buster Higgins
Jane Elizabeth Higgins
Jennifer Hills
Maggie Hingston
Joanne Hodgson

Neil Hodgson

Rachel Holdsworth

Amber Hollingworth-Hoegg

Andy Hollyhead

Emily Hopkins

Rosie Hopkins

Kate Hughes

Holly Huish

Ken Hunnisett

Alistair Huston

Sarah Hyde

Claire Innes

Rivka Isaacson

Johari Ismail

Paul Jackson

Michael Jardine

Karolien Jaspers

Leonie Jennings

Sam Jennings

Titus Jennings

Dan Leinir Turthra Jensen

Adam Johansen

Ashley John

David Johnson

Dee Johnson

Nancy Johnston

Rhona Johnstone

Conal Jones

Hannah Jones

Deborah Jones-Davis

SUBSCRIBERS

Daniel Jordan
Henning Michael Just
Milan Juza
Susanne Kahle
Philip Marcel Karré
Jonathan Kaufman
Noel Keane
Susanna Keeley
Sarah Keeling
Charlotte Keep
Gillian Kern
Audrey Keszek
Dan Kieran
Ellie King
Simon King
Amy Kingswell
Olivia Knibbs
Annette Knight
Anne Kupschus
Pierre L'Allier
Andreas Lammers
Lang
Kerstin Langdon
Belinda Ledgerton
Ian Leslie
Elizabeth Leven
Claire Lickman
Holly Linklater
Kim Locke
Katherine Lockwood

Sarah Longair
Alex Lovell-Troy
Stuart Lowbridge
David Ludlow
Lisa Lyons
Jen Malicka
Philippa Manasseh
Stephanie Mantell
Shuna Marr
Anne Marte Hvalby
Simon Maylott
Sophie McAllister
Emma McClain
Joe McCormack
Rachael McKelvey
Palma McKeown
Drew McMillan
Tom McPhillips
Caroline Meier
Ingo Friedrich Meyer
Colin Midson
Sophie Milton
Daniel Mitchell
John Mitchinson
Tom Moody-Stuart
Ned Morrell
Anna Moss
Jennifer Moss
Liane Mount
Asya Muchnick

Keith Poulton
Rachel Poulton
Denise Price
Kieran Prout
Lisa Ravenscroft
Lizzie Read
Amanda Redhead
Adina Reeve
Mark Richards
Emma Rigby
Jo Rodgers
Al Roots
Laura & Emma Rouffiac
Thorsten Ruffle-Brandt
Lisa Rull
Alison Rutter
Alexandra Scannell
Aïsha Schofield
Robyn Scott
Paul Scullion
Matthew Searle
Valerie Selby
Lynette Sherburne
Ben Simmonite
Heather Simmonite
Kate Sinar
Kim Sirag
Claire Slade
Jennifer Smith
Christie Snyder
Emma Southerington

A NOTE ON THE TYPEFACES

The body text is set in Ehrhardt, a typeface developed in 1937 by Stanley Morison while at the Monotype Corporation. Morison was responsible for making modern versions of many antique faces, including Bembo and Baskerville, and designed the now ubiquitous Times New Roman. The creator of the original Ehrhardt typeface is unknown but it is named after the late seventeenth-century Ehrhardt foundry in Leipzig, and is similar to some Dutch typefaces of that period produced by the Amsterdam printer Anton Janson. The typographical historian Robin Nicholas believes Ehrhardt was Morison's take on Janson, 'made a little heavier and narrower to give improved legibility and economy'.

The headings are set in Bauer Bodoni, a version of the famous eighteenth-century typeface that was re-drawn in 1926. Giambattista Bodoni (1740–1813) was known as 'the king of typographers and the typographer of kings', because of his well-heeled clientele. He personally designed and engraved 298 typefaces in his lifetime and when he died a red scar caused by the bar of his printing press was found across his chest. William Morris believed Bodoni was the 'most illegible type that was ever cut . . . owing to the clumsy thickening and vulgar thinning of the line'.

xxΩ